HARD DISCIPLINE

LESSONS IN DOMINANCE

JACKIE ASHENDEN

SC PRESS

Copyright © 2025 by Jackie Ashenden

All rights reserved.

No part of this book may be reproduced in any form or by any electronic or mechanical means, including information storage and retrieval systems, without written permission from the author, except for the use of brief quotations in a book review.

My boyfriend can't give me what I want...but his dad can give me the dominance I crave.

Odette

My relationship with my boyfriend is fizzling out. I can't give him what he wants, if I don't even know what I want. That's why I sign up for The Club app. It's guaranteed to help you explore your fantasies - safely and anonymously. I may have told a little white lie about my experience level - but I'm confident that I can handle whatever discipline my match decides to give me. But when I show up at the hotel for my first scene, I know the man waiting for me. My boyfriend's dad.

Gideon

Ever since my wife's death I only want it one way - anonymous, and with me in total control. I'm not a nice, soft dom. Quite the opposite. I'm definitely not the one for a woman looking to try submission for the first time. But that's not the biggest problem I have with the woman who just walked into my hotel room. Odette is my son's girlfriend. I'm not the world's best dad, but even I'm not that bad. But when I try to send her away, we end up entangled in something hotter than either of us bargained for. Our age gap is too big, and I'm too scarred to ever give her what she wants. But after one night together, I can't let her go...

Look for other books in the Lessons in Dominance series: AFTER HOURS by Caitlin Crews, BOUND AND BRANDED by Maisey Yates, BAD GIRL DILEMMA by Zara Cox.

1

Odette

The Uber drops me off right in front of the huge glass edifice that is The Clouds, Manhattan's newest and most exclusive hotel, and I hate it on sight. It's a monument to rich men and greed, and also it's kind of phallic. I'm sure a man designed it.

I struggle to pull down the hem of my too-short black dress as I get out of the car at the same time as I'm trying to balance on the cheap black patent heels I bought online a couple of years ago and never wear. I'm also second-guessing myself as to why I'm here, but hey, at least I *am* here. I've been working on my follow-through, which, and I'll be the first to admit, I'm not great at. But still, I'm out of my apartment so that's something.

My mom named me Odette after the princess in Swan Lake, which I do not love. It doesn't help that I have long pale hair and am built on the small side, so people think I'm either a victim or a princess—AKA too helpless to look after myself. Which isn't true. To be honest, I wish I was built taller, stronger, and more muscular than I am, but I'm a woman and we're never happy with the body we're born with. I could have gone to the gym, I guess, but that would involve being around strangers and I'm not good with strangers—so weak, with noodle arms, it is.

On the sidewalk outside the hotel, the doormen nod as I approach, and one holds the door open for me. I wonder who they think I am in my obviously cheap clothing. A sex worker, probably, though I'm not as well dressed as, say, a high-class escort would be. Still, I was told I'd be expected so at least I don't have to plead with them to let me in.

Inside, everything is black marble and gold, the reception desk a huge slab of the same black marble as the floor. A man sits behind it, wearing black, and as I open my mouth to say I'm an expected guest, he points me towards one of the elevators.

Okay then. I close my mouth and walk over to it, nervously clutching my glittery silver evening purse, which now feels like the wrong choice.

My God, I hate places like this, which is a little rich coming from someone currently dating the son of a billionaire, I know, but still. This is not my natural habitat and it shows. It makes me feel conspicuous, and if there's one thing I hate, it's feeling conspicuous.

The elevator doors open and I search the for button I need. The instructions said that I was to meet him in the Pinnacle Suite and sure enough, there's a button just for that suite. So I press it. The elevator doors close and we're moving.

So, okay, the reason I'm here is not for sex work (which is fine, I'm not judging), but sex. Just sex. I signed up to this app called The Club, which is kind of like a dating service for people into BDSM, and I've been matched with some guy called Master Six. This is what they term a "playdate" but obviously this kind of playdate isn't for kids.

I did a lot of research before deciding The Club was the way to go, so it wasn't like a spur of the moment thing. Sure, I don't know this guy from Adam — his bio was only a list of things he's into and there was no picture — which is usually a giant no from me, but The Club members are vetted and clinic visits are mandatory, so he's probably not a psycho. I kind of lied on my own bio, though. I said I was an experienced submissive, but I'm not. I've actually never done any BDSM before, so what I'm doing tonight is probably going to end up being a giant mistake, but oh well. *C'est la vie.* I'm not backing out, not now.

I was assaulted last year while I was in college (Yale if you must know). I was out with some girlfriends and I left the bar early because I needed to study, and I didn't notice the guy following me. He shoved me up against a wall and punched me in the face and then...yeah, it's all still a blur. Anyway, I've always been anxious, but the assault pushed my anxiety into a full blown panic disorder, and eventually I ended up dropping out of college. I was there on a scholarship, so that was a bummer, but even more so was the six months I spent in my apartment, not wanting to leave it. I'm much better now — I got some therapy and the panic attacks are under control — but I'm not where I want to be.

My relationship with my boyfriend, Lucas, isn't going well. He's a nice guy, but he didn't sign up to babysit a poor, frightened mouse, and I'm really conscious of that. He's never said anything, but ever since the assault he treats me as if I'm made of glass, and even though I told him he didn't need to, he still does. Especially in bed, which is where the main issue is. He touches me as if I might break, constantly asking me if I'm okay, which makes me *more* anxious not less. I feel as if he's the one who's not okay and I'm the one having to give him reassurance, which isn't fair, because he's trying. But still, it's not sexy for me and it makes it difficult to get lost in the moment.

Anyway, I wouldn't have done anything about it if it wasn't for Gideon Fairfax.

He's Lucas's dad and I met him for the first time last summer at the Fairfax Estate in the Hamptons. He's some kind of property billionaire, and Lucas has a problematic relationship with him, because after Lucas's mother died, his father basically pulled away and buried himself in work.

So far, so terrible, billionaire dad.

But that's not the worst part. The worst part, the really, *really*, like, terrible part, is that Lucas's dad is the hottest fucking man I've ever laid eyes on. I should also say *not including Lucas* but I can't say that because he's hotter than his son. He's got that older man vibe, where men kind of settle into their looks and what was once pretty, becomes harder, stronger, edgier. Also, he's just got this...aura about him. It's the confidence of a man at the top of his game, a man with money and power, a leader through and through. He has a presence, a charisma, a magnetism, a....

I don't know... Something that you can't put into words, that you can only feel.

Anyway, the day Lucas introduced me to him, Mr. Fairfax's startling blue eyes met mine and I forgot what I was going to say. I just stood there gawping at him like a fish trying to breathe air. He shook my hand, said something about being pleased to meet me, then asked me where I was from. I couldn't remember how to speak so he had to ask me twice. So fucking embarrassing. But I could have gotten used to him and his effect on me, if it hadn't been for the incident with the horse. Some girl was riding on the beach below the Fairfax estate and a dog startled her horse. Lucas and I had been sunbathing, and I'd looked up at the barking dog just as Mr. Fairfax was coming out of the water. So I had a front row seat to him taking control of the horse situation. He grabbed the reins and ran one large hand down its neck and flanks, his deep voice issuing firm orders. He was only in swimming trunks, but he may as well have been wearing a crown for all that impaired his air of command.

Meanwhile, I sat there, my mouth open, staring at the expanse of smooth, olive skin wet from the sea, the sunlight shining on the water sheening every perfect muscle of his body. And my God....what a body it was. I never knew anyone's dad could look like that, but Lucas's dad did.

That night, in bed with Lucas, I tried to get him to be a little firmer with me, tell me what he wanted me to do, that kind of thing, but he didn't understand. So I had to get myself off after he'd fallen asleep, guiltily imagining I was the skittish horse, with Mr. Fairfax's strong hands on me, his voice telling me what to do...

Anyway, months of fantasies and continually disappointing sex with Lucas later, things between us are going downhill fast, and I need to do something to fix it. I mean, the problem is me, and I can't tell Lucas what I want, because I don't really know.

Hence me signing up to The Club. I get off on dominating fantasies featuring Mr. Fairfax, so what I want by signing up is to find out if I'm actually submissive. And if I am, that means that I can tell Lucas what I need, instead of him trying to guess. But obviously I need someone experienced, someone I can trust, and that's why I got The Club app.

The elevator stops and the doors slide open, revealing a silent, peaceful looking sitting area with a low couch and a table with a single orchid artistically arranged in a glass vase. To the right as I step from the elevator car, is a door. A gold plaque on the wall beside it tells me that this is indeed the Pinnacle Suite and a book has been put between the door and the frame to stop it from closing.

He said the door would be open and I should just walk in.

I swallow, my anxiety getting worse as I stare at the door standing ajar.

I shouldn't have lied on my application form when I joined The Club. You're supposed to put in your bio if you're new to the scene, or only interested in exploring, but I didn't. Because the other reason I'm here is that I didn't want anyone to treat me like I'm made of glass or go easy on me. I want to feel strong, have someone silence the constant hum of anxiety in my brain, and maybe Master Six will do that for me. I fucking hope so, because if this doesn't work, I don't know what I'll do.

I keep staring at the door, not moving. Turns out that thinking a thing is fine, but when it comes time to doing it, then it's a whole different story. Still, I've managed to get myself this far, so falling at the first hurdle would be dumb.

I take a steadying breath and make myself walk through the front door of the suite, letting it close behind me.

It's deathly quiet inside. In front of me is a very short hallway, so I walk down it, my heart thumping, the heels of my pumps sinking into the thick, cream carpet. The whole place reeks of luxury on a level I can't even begin to imagine; clearly Master Six isn't short of cash.

I step out of the hallway and into a huge living area dominated by big plate glass windows. They're massive and since the curtains aren't drawn, all of Central Park rolls out before us like a thick dark carpet dotted with lights. The room itself has a chandelier hanging from the ceiling, the same thick cream carpet as the hall and a huge modular couch in pale velvet facing the windows. A gigantic TV hangs on one wall, with yet more seating in front of it, and on the opposite side of the room is a long sideboard with lots of shelves and drawers.

A man is standing in front of it with his back to me. He's pouring drinks. He's very tall and from the way the plain black cotton of his business shirt stretches across wide, muscular shoulders, he's clearly built. He's wearing black pants and I can't help but notice that his waist is narrow and his thighs powerful. His hair is short and black, and as he deals with the drinks, his movements are unhurried.

Interest flickers inside me. I didn't give much thought to what kind of guy Master Six would be, or whether he'd be hot. I was too busy overthinking my impulsive agreement to meet him. But now I'm here and so is he, and he looks like he should be in a boxing ring or maybe charging across a battlefield with an axe, and hell, I'm only human. I only hope he's as hot from the front as he is from the back.

He doesn't turn and he doesn't speak, though he must know I'm here, and my anxiety intensifies. I should announce myself, but I'm sure my voice will shake and that's not a great first impression. Besides, there's a strange familiarity to him that's tugging at me and I don't know why.

I frown, studying his powerful figure as he calmly drops ice cubes into one of the tumblers. No, I'm not sure what about him is familiar, and that's a good thing since no one knows what I'm doing right now and I don't want anyone to know, either. Especially not Lucas, because obviously this is cheating. Even though I'm doing it *for* him. For us, really.

After all, it's not like I'm going to do this again. This is very definitely a one-time thing.

I finally muster up the courage to announce myself, since it seems this guy isn't going to say anything anytime soon, but as soon as I open my mouth, he says, "You're late." He drops more ice cubes into the second glass. They make a metallic clinking sound. "Take your clothes off then go and kneel by the windows."

His voice is deep, dark as night, with a roughness to it that strokes over my skin like a cat's tongue. It's familiar, so, *so* familiar, and the coldest of shocks go through me as I realize why.

It's Gideon Fairfax's voice. Which must mean that this man is Gideon Fairfax.

Lucas's dad.

Fuck.

I freeze. I'm dead. Deceased. Just completely inanimate. A husk. My brain is screaming, *It's fucking Lucas's fucking dad!* over and over.

It can't be him, it can't be. But what if it is? What do I do? Stay here? Run from the room screaming from the room like a fucking lunatic? A little of both?

I need to get out, move, disappear before he turns around, but he's turning and I know already that it's too late. My body tenses, ready to go, but it's as if everything has dropped into slo-mo as Gideon Fairfax finishes his turn, and yes, it's him.

And yes, I'm fucked.

Totally fucked.

2

Gideon

Jesus Christ and all the fucking saints. What the fuck is my son's pale waif of a girlfriend doing here? In *my* fucking hotel room? I'm expecting company, yes, but it's supposed to be a woman who goes by the name of Artemis, a new and experienced member of The Club. Her bio caught my eye because although she didn't have a profile picture, she was new and since I've gotten a little bored of the subs currently on offer, I messaged her to see if she was up for a playdate. She had tonight free and so I'm waiting for her, not Odette fucking Bishop, for Christ's sake.

Odette is standing there staring at me, her silvery gray eyes wide with shock. She's in a tight black minidress and cheap, black patent stripper heels, and she's clutching a glittery silver purse like a mountain climber clutches an ice axe to keep himself from falling. Her white-blonde hair has been caught in a smooth, high ponytail, which is always nice since it gives me something to hold onto—

Wait. The fuck? Why the hell am I thinking that?

"M-Mr. F-F-Fairfax?" she stutters, her husky voice hoarse with surprise. "W-What are you doing here?"

I've got nothing against Odette. She's small and delicate, and pretty, but she looks as if a stiff breeze would blow her away and quite frankly, I thought Lucas's tastes ran to Amazons, not Tinkerbell. Apparently they met at Yale, so she must have a head on her shoulders, but the first time I met her she was so shy she could barely string two words together. Lucas is a cocky little asshole, pulling all the cheerleaders — at least he did in high school — so privately I was surprised at his choice of this colorless looking child. But my relationship with my son is strained at the best of times, so I kept those thoughts to myself.

Anyway, I've barely said two words to the girl, so fuck knows what she's doing here. I cannot fathom it.

"What do you mean 'what am I doing here'?" I say tersely. "This is *my* hotel room. The real question is what are *you* doing in it?"

She swallows, her slender fingers moving nervously on her purse as if it's a slippery rock she's trying to find purchase on. "I...I...um. I'm s-supposed to meet someone."

I lean back against the sideboard and fold my arms. "In this suite? In this hotel? *My* fucking hotel?"

Her eyes get even wider, even rounder. "This is your hotel?"

Christ, has Lucas not told her what I do for a living? "Yes. I own Fairfax Hotels, which built this building. Luc didn't tell you?"

She opens and closes her mouth as if searching for words and for some reason I find myself staring. She's

Hard Discipline

wearing red lipstick, which I haven't seen on her before, and it sharply outlines a pair of full, pouty lips. "I...I m-mean, maybe. I can't....I mean, I don't..." She makes a feeble gesture with one hand. "So...um...no."

Fuck's sake. I need her out of here and now, before Artemis arrives, though speaking of, she's ten minutes late and that means less playtime for me, which is irritating. I need this tonight. It's Gabrielle's birthday and even though it's been ten years since she died, anniversaries are still difficult for me.

These playdates with women from The Club are one way I deal with her loss, letting out the side of me that likes control, that demands it. With a sub I can lose myself for a couple of hours, let off some steam, and simply be in the moment, at least for a little while. Easier than a hookup, which requires explanations and all kinds of other emotional bullshit I don't have the bandwidth for these days.

Odette is looking nervously at me and shifting on her feet, and I can't for the life of me understand how she knew I was here and that the door would be open and—

Wait. A creeping suspicion begins to wind through me and every single muscle in my body tenses. "Tell me why you're here," I order quietly, firmly, in the tone I use during a domination scene. "Now."

Her gaze wavers at the demand in my voice, and she takes a frantic little breath. Then the words all rush out, piling on top of one another. "I-I'm here to meet a man called Master Six who I was matched with on—"

I hold up my hand and she stops talking. My body is cold with disappointment. Fucking hell. Odette Bishop cannot be Artemis, that's just not possible. Except she's looking at me the way a rabbit looks at a fox and something inside me is telling me that not only is it possible, it's the truth.

So I ask her, flat out. "Are you Artemis?"

She swallows yet again, her knuckles white as she clutches that damn purse. "Y-Yes."

"Jesus Christ." The words escape before I can stop them, my disappointment intensifying. If she's Artemis, then it looks like my playdate will not be happening tonight, which is not acceptable. "You signed up through The Club?" I ask, just to make sure.

Slowly, she nods, her eyes round as silver coins.

Fuck's sake. I dig into my pocket and get out my phone, opening up the app. I'm going to have to cancel this date, then find someone else, which will be difficult at such short notice. It's either that or I go to a club downtown, but I prefer to conduct my playdates in the privacy of a hotel room. I'm not worried that people might find out my predilections, it's just that I'm a controlling prick and I like to be the only one in charge.

I let out a breath, ignoring the pull of disappointment and the cold grief that lies beneath it, and try to be nice. "Well, I'm sure you have questions, but I'm afraid now is not the time. So why don't you run along, Miss Bishop. We need never speak of this again."

I expect her to do as she's told, except she doesn't. She only stands there, staring at me with big eyes, her mouth full and fire-engine red. "I'm not cheating on him," she blurts out. "Not really. I just wanted to know if I liked it. That's it. That's all."

Jesus, who does she think I am? Her confessor?

"You mean Lucas, presumably?" I don't wait for answer because I know it already. "I don't give a fuck if you're

3

Odette

I'm still trembling inside, but the whisky is settling in my stomach and the burst of shock that went through me the moment I saw his face— that turned to anger as he basically ran a sword through my relationship with Lucas— has intensified, drowning my previous anxiety. All I can think is *fuck him*. It was *so* hard to get here, he can't possibly understand just how hard, and I won't be dismissed like a child. I just won't.

I know I stood there gaping at him like a fucking idiot the minute he turned around, and yes, that Master Six is also apparently Mr. Fairfax, made the whole weird situation even weirder and even more embarrassing, but what with the whole shock thing and then my brain screaming at me, I just couldn't move.

Then when it became clear to him that I was Artemis

usually doesn't bother me when it comes to subs, it's certainly bothering me now.

"Stop looking at me like that," I order. "And get the fuck out."

She doesn't move, continuing to stand there, staring at the carpet.

So. This girl has some guts to her after all.

Then just when I think I'm going to have physically pick her up and dump her in the hall outside, she abruptly comes towards me, her gaze still averted. She reaches for one of the tumblers of scotch I poured in preparation for my evening and before I can say anything she knocks it back, including the ice, then slams the tumbler back down and stares at me.

"I'm not going to be able to do this again," she says almost furiously. "It took everything I had just to walk through the fucking door and I'm not leaving now. So, Mr. Fairfax. Are we going to do this or not?"

he's showing no interest in crossing it. I don't blame him for that, not when it's my fault, but I'm not getting into the complexities of that, not with this pale, colorless girl.

"The relationship I have with my son is none of your fucking business," I say coldly. "Now get out before I throw you out."

She continues to stare at me fixedly, then puts her narrow shoulders back, drawing herself up. And there's something in her eyes, a silvery flicker of heat, that for some reason makes my breath catch.

The feeling is so unexpected that this time I'm the one staring at her as if I've never seen her before in my entire life. She's small and delicate and yes, very pretty. Strands of pale hair have escaped her ponytail and they're curling around her ears. Her dress is very close fitting, revealing small, rounded breasts, narrow waist, and the slight curve of her hips. Her eye lashes and brows are pale, but her mouth is deliciously red.

I like my women built strong enough to take what I give out, and she's definitely not one of those women, yet…

Color blooms in her pale cheeks and she blinks, tearing her gaze from mine, and I feel it like a punch to the gut. A kick of raw heat. The dominant in me abruptly taking an interest. I like the way she can't hold my gaze and how nervous she is. Nervous little subs quivering at my approach are, in fact, my favorite. It shows that they're hyper aware of me, their minds twisting and turning as they try to guess what I might do. So I make sure to never do what they expect, which intensifies their pleasure and in turn, my power. Mind games, fuck, I can't get enough.

But not with this one. She's not only my son's girlfriend, she's twenty years younger than me, and while an age gap cheating on him. He's a grown man, he can look after himself."

A crease appears between her pale brows, an expression of concern on her pretty face. "You don't care about him?"

Great, this is the last thing I either need or want, a discussion with my son's girlfriend about my son's love life. The really sad thing is that I suspect Lucas is tired of her and doesn't know how to tell her.

"I do care about him," I say before adding, because my son doesn't know how to end a relationship, "but the fact is, he's not in love with you, Odette. You're not his type." It's cruel of me to say this to her face, but the ugly truth is kinder than many a pretty lie. And it *is* the truth. Lucas isn't in love with her, because if he was, she wouldn't be making BDSM dates on a sex app.

Odette's gaze wavers and I see something that looks like hurt glitter there. It doesn't bother me, I'm expecting her to be hurt. But then hurt vanishes and it's replaced by something I didn't expect. Anger. Which is interesting. Seems she has a bit of spirit after all.

"How do you know what his type is?" she says without stammering once. "When he's barely seen you for the past five years."

The barb is unexpected and hits me straight in the chest. Another ugly truth. After Gabrielle died, the only thing that kept the grief at bay was work and so I dived head first into it. My heart was ashes and I had nothing left to give Luc, especially not the kind of support a grieving teenager needed. I told myself I was giving him space, that he didn't need my grief on top of his own, and it's a lie I've been telling myself for the past ten years. Grief made me selfish, and now it's too late. There's distance between us, a distance *I* put there, and (my stupid handle in the app), his look first of shock, then second, disappointment, hit me like a kick from a mule. And something woke inside me, a lost, angry part of myself that had been sleeping since the attack. Before I knew what I was doing I'd opened my mouth and a whole lot of stupid words had come flooding out. He'd been unmoved, because of course he was. But I couldn't stand there, listening to him tell me how Lucas wasn't in love with me and that I wasn't his type. I wasn't that much of a doormat. Lucas had told me many times how distant his father was and how he preferred working to spending time with his son, and so I couldn't help pointing that out to him.

I mean, I knew that Lucas didn't love me already, but there was no need for his father to rub it in. Then telling me to get the fuck out, when it had taken all my meager courage to even get here had been the last straw. Apparently grabbing a whisky tumbler and swallowing the whole lot, then demanding an answer about whether we were going to do this or not, was the thing I needed to do.

It was a mistake, but I didn't understand that until now, because *now* I'm standing close to him and he's beside me, dwarfing me with his height. He's like a redwood to my bonsai, except redwood trees don't have eyes the intense blue of lapis lazuli, or a face that looks as if God himself has carved it. He's got slightly winged dark brows, a fierce blade of a nose, and a drop-dead beautiful mouth. There are lines around that mouth and those eyes, and he has white at his temples, and a slight salt and pepper scatter to the stubble on his strong jaw, but all those things just make him sexier. He's got the first two buttons of his shirt undone and I can't stop staring at the olive skin of his throat, remembering him mostly naked on the beach, where I could see more than his throat. I shiver, watching his pulse there. It's regular and strong, unlike mine, racing like a terrified rabbit under my skin.

"This?" he demands in that deep, sexy-as-hell voice. "What the fuck are you talking about?"

I swallow, hypnotized by the column of his throat and neck, trying to remember what words are. "Uh...um...you know...."

"Eyes up."

I obey without thought, lifting my gaze to the blue of his eyes. They pierce me the same way they did the summer I met him, making me want to drown myself in them.

"What. The. Fuck. Are. You. Talking. About?" He enunciates each word, biting them off as if each one is a coin from his hoard that he doesn't want to give away.

The angry part of me bristles, because goddamn it's patronizing.

"You. Know. What. I'm. Talking. About." I say, mimicking him before I can think better of it. "BDMS."

"BDSM," he corrects. "Do you even know what that means?"

I flush. "Yes, of course. I did my research before I signed up."

His gaze narrows. "But you've never done it before, have you?"

"Of course," I repeat far too quickly, and once the words are out of my mouth, the flush in my cheeks deepens, betraying the lie.

He says nothing for a long moment, his gaze searing in the same way the back end of a rocket is searing. I want desperately to look away, but I want to show him he can't intimidate me, so I don't.

"Listen," he says finally, his voice hard. "There are a

million different reasons why this is not happening, not least of which is that you lied in your bio, but here's another to add to the pile. I'm not into training new submissives. I want someone experienced and you are not it."

Wow, okay then. He's not a man who minces words. He purees them. Lucas did mention that his father wasn't a nice man and he's certainly making no allowances for me.

Isn't that what you wanted?

Well, yes, it is, but I can't deny that it also stings a little. Though really, he's got every right to be annoyed. The woman he thought he was getting tonight isn't the woman he thought he was getting tonight and he's pissed about it.

I take a breath, trying to calm the rushing beat of my heart. Okay, so, he doesn't want me here, that's obvious, and he probably isn't attracted to me in the slightest, not the way I am to him, but I can't leave now, not when it took so much of myself to get here.

You should leave. Luc will hate it if he ever finds out what you've been doing.

Yeah, I know. I shouldn't keep standing here. I shouldn't push myself on a man who clearly isn't interested and who is, yes, Luc's fucking dad. And yes, Luc will definitely hate it should he ever find out. And I could find myself another match on The Club, though I'm not sure I'll be able to force myself to do this a second time....

But....

He's just looking at me and I can see anger flickering in his eyes, and he's so fucking hot, and now I know that he's into this whole BDSM thing... God all I can think about is the way he spoke to that horse, his voice very firm, his hand stroking the horse's heaving sides, and how slowly the animal settled.

Would I do that if he spoke firmly to me? If he stroked

me with those large, blunt-fingered hands? Would the frantic whirling of my anxious brain be finally silenced? God, this is so messed up. *I'm* so messed up.

"Okay," I say shakily, still trapped by the blue of his gaze. "So, you're right. I'm not experienced. But I really want—"

"I don't care what you really want," he interrupts in a voice as hard as granite. "I'm not into young women and I don't do training. If that's what you want then you'll have to look for another Master. Alternatively..." He pauses and his gaze becomes impossibly sharper. "You could have a direct conversation with my son about what you want."

My face flames as the embarrassment of him knowing what I want comes crashing down on me again. It's not that I'm ashamed of it, it's just...uncomfortable. Which is why I wanted to do this with a complete stranger. But of course, now he knows, so I force myself to reply, "I've tried. But the problem is that I don't really know what I want. I only know what I don't want."

"Then tell him that," Mr. Fairfax says. "Not me."

"He's too gentle with me," I continue, running at the mouth because no matter the embarrassment, that's apparently what I do now. "He keeps asking me if I'm okay all the time, and can he touch me here or there, or is he hurting me and it makes me feel as if it's my job to reassure *him* all the time. I can't stand it."

A silence falls as the last word leaves my lips and instantly I want to sink through the luxurious cream carpet and into the room below. Why the fuck did I say all of that? *My God, find yourself a proper sex therapist, Odette. Don't stand there oversharing with your potential father-in-law.*

If Mr. Fairfax finds what I've said as embarrassing as I do, he gives no sign. In fact, I'm starting to wonder if he ever gets embarrassed. Probably not. Which is somehow comforting, weirdly enough. I breathe in his scent, something warm, cedar and sandalwood, so different to the sharpness of salt and citrus that Lucas prefers. It's calming that scent, and something in me gets slightly less tense.

"I don't like having to repeat myself," he says. "But again, Odette. You're having this conversation with the wrong man. You should be talking to my son."

He's right, I should, but that angry, stubborn part of me won't let it go. I've been afraid for too long, constantly fighting my anxiety, and I'm tired of it. The attack on me was random, I was in the wrong place at the wrong time, but my brain refuses to accept that. It goes over it and over it, trying to fill in the gaps in my memory. He hit me, but what else did he do? Was I sexually assaulted? There was no evidence of it, but since I can't remember, the lack of memory haunts me. And they never caught him, so in addition to going over and over it, trying to think about what I could have done differently, I also see his face in every man I meet.

I want it to stop. I want to feel something other than fear and I have the sense that while it might be messed up, Gideon Fairfax can give that to me. So no, I'm not leaving yet.

I reach for the other tumbler of scotch, desperate for more courage, but as quickly as I reach for it, his hand is there, long, blunt fingers wrapping around my wrist, gripping it. "No," he growls. "No more alcohol."

My breath catches hard in my throat and I freeze, his hand like a shackle around my wrist. His fingers are warm and strong, his grip firm. I wouldn't be able to pull away from him even if I wanted to, and I don't know why but that thought is insanely hot. I stare at floor, my breathing getting faster and faster, my heart hammering in my ears.

Yet another silence falls, but this time there's a tension to it, an electricity I've never felt before. He's looking at me, I know it. I can feel his gaze like a pressure on the top of my head, and my awareness expands, taking in the tall, powerful body so close to mine. His heat. His tantalizing scent.

I'm trembling all of a sudden, but for the first time in years, it's not with fear. I can hardly believe that it's desire, since I can't remember when I last felt it so strongly, but the ache between my thighs seems to indicate that yes, indeed, it's desire. Mr. Fairfax is only gripping my wrist and looking at me, yet I'm so turned on I can hardly speak, and all I can think is that Lucas never made me feel like this. Not once.

His grip tightens minutely and I catch my breath, adrenaline pouring through me, but then—shocking me—he lets me go. Disappointment slides through me like a splinter of ice, and I look up at him, because surely the way his grip tightened meant something. Surely....

Except his gaze is hard as it meets mine. "You don't want what I have to give, Odette. Believe me, you don't."

I take a shuddering breath. "How do you know?"

"Because you're a child."

"I'm not," I say, still trembling all over, my voice husky. "Show me."

He's tense and muscle flicks in his jaw; he's angry. Disappointed, clearly, that his promised submissive for the evening has turned out to be his son's girlfriend, who is now making demands of him.

"Show you what?" His voice is like granite.

"Show me what you have to give," I say. "Then I'll know if I want it or not."

His expression is impassive, but his eyes glitter. "No."

I swallow. "Please."

"No." There is no give in his voice, none at all.

But I can't let this go, I just can't, and before I realize what I'm doing, I drop to my knees at his feet. I stare at the black polished leather of his shoes and remember what a good submissive is supposed to say. "Please," I whisper. "Sir."

4

Gideon

Odette's pale head is bent, the very picture of a good sub. Whether she knows it or not, that desperation in her voice is a real fucking problem because a desperate, pleading sub is my goddamn catnip. Then, of course, the icing on the cake, that soft little *Please, Sir*.

I'm a hardline Dom and I demand a lot of my subs, which is why I like them experienced. But this girl, kneeling at my feet, wouldn't last two seconds in a scene with me and I know that for a fact. Shit, I said no for a reason and I meant it.

So, really, I should not, under any circumstances, even be contemplating giving her what she wants. Her hair is so pale, though, a pretty white-blonde with a black elastic band holding her ponytail in place.

It would feel soft. Soft, like her skin...

I grit my teeth. I shouldn't have grabbed her wrist when she reached for that whisky tumbler, but instinct kicked in before I could think better of it. She shouldn't be drinking any more alcohol, especially since she's already downed one. Being so slight even one drink might put her under the table. But stopping her meant touching her and now I know what her skin feels like, smooth and silky and soft. Now I also know how my touch affects her. She'd trembled as I'd gripped her, the race of her pulse beating hard under my fingertips. I like knowing that it was me that made it race. Me, that made her tremble.

I can't deny that making a woman desperate is a powerful aphrodisiac. I've always liked it. I never played dominance games with Gabrielle, though, because that wasn't on my radar back then. I was bossy in bed, nothing more than that, but even then nothing got me off more than when she begged me to make her come. It wasn't until after she died that I got into BDSM. A lover introduced me and immediately I threw myself into it, because it was different from the sex I'd had with Gabrielle and that's what I'd wanted back then. Something that had nothing to do with her, had no memories of her, and was nothing she'd ever want. It was sex that I could enjoy without her ghost haunting me. Also, I very much enjoyed how in control and powerful it made me feel, the perfect antidote to how weak and powerless I was when I lost her.

But it only works with someone who won't demand any emotional involvement. I have subs I play with on a semi-regular basis, but they're women who don't want anything more than to get off and who don't need much in the way of aftercare.

Which means it will not work with this woman. Hell,

even if she wasn't my son's girlfriend, I wouldn't touch her for her inexperience alone.

My jaw aches as I stare down at her bent head.

Show me, she'd said, as if I was a magician and she wanted to know how the trick was done. But there is no trick, only complete obedience to my will, and I don't think she'd like that one bit.

I can hear her taking fast gulps of air, and I can see she's still trembling. I've denied her and denied her, but she's pushing in the way a sub pushes, using her own obedience to get me to give her what she wants, and that is not something I allow

She needs to be taught a lesson.

The Dominant in me stirs and I find myself falling into the space where I'm analytical, studying the sub to find out what her weak points are and where her vulnerabilities lie. She overshared about Lucas and how he treats her, and it doesn't surprise me. He's trying to do the right thing, but he's impatient in the way all young men are impatient. He wants to get straight to the fucking without understanding that sometimes the fucking is not the goal. It's the cherry on top. But she didn't like his questions, she said. She didn't like him asking her if she was okay all the time.

You know what she needs.

I have an inkling. But it's not what she wants, because wants and needs are two different things. She thinks what she wants are a few power games, a bit of light bondage, one or two orders, but that's not what she needs. I'm certain of it. And that's not what I provide.

Show her the difference then.

Perhaps. Perhaps I should. If I show her the hard, cold reality of what being my sub means, shock her with it, she'll understand why it will never happen with me. Never.

I reach down to touch the top of her head, testing her. She takes a sharp breath at the brush of my fingertips, and I don't like how it goes straight to my head like a shot of good whisky.

I love that nervousness in a sub, that little shiver of apprehension when I approach. It's not fear of me so much as it's fear of what I'll make her do, fear that she'll do it without question and, more than that, that she'll love it. And they *do* love it. No sub ever leaves me unsatisfied.

She's pushy, this one, and won't take no for an answer, but after five minutes with me she won't be so quick to insist. I'll scare her back to vanilla sex for life.

Her hair is very soft and I curl my fingers around the base of her ponytail, gripping it. She draws in another sharp breath. She's trembling, I can feel it.

My cock twitches, anticipating what's next, but I'm not going to give it what it wants, not tonight. If she wasn't Lucas's girlfriend, I might consider fucking her — sometimes I don't fuck my subs, it depends on how well behaved they are — but there's no changing who she is, or who I am. I've been a shitty father to my son, but I'm not *that* shitty.

You really think not *fucking her makes it better?*

No, it doesn't, I'm not that naive. But she's a problem, and it's clear she wants me, so if I don't want her to become more of a problem I'll have to nip her little explorations in the bud. Now.

Her ponytail feels good in my palm and I like how responsive she is. There's something undeniably erotic about how new this is for her, and that surprises me. I didn't think I was into it, but clearly I'm wrong. She probably hasn't experienced anything like this before, all the sensations and feelings so bright and sharp and hot...

Shit. No, I can't think of her as my sub. I can't get into her head, wanting to know what she's thinking and feeling. That's not what I'd decided. What I've decided is fifteen minutes of my own particular brand of domination and that's all.

"You want me to show you?" I ask into the silence. "I can do that. But first, you need answer three questions and answer them honestly or else this doesn't happen." This is something I do with all the subs I play with. It's become a little ritual of mine and though I don't need to ask my questions of the subs on The Club app, I like to hear the answers anyway. It helps get them into the moment and makes them focus on me.

She lets out a shaken breath and then nods her head.

"I need you to speak." My voice has deepened, hardened, the Dominant in me coming out to play. "I need to hear the words."

"Y-Yes," she finally whispers.

"Good. First question. Do you want this?"

"Yes," she says quickly and without a stammer. "Oh God, yes."

The note of hunger in the words makes my cock harden in response, but again, I ignore it. Controlling my body is second nature to me after so many years. "Next question. Do you trust me?"

For the first time she hesitates. "Trust you? What do you mean?"

"BDSM only works if we trust each other completely." I don't normally explain myself to a sub — it's all part of the mind games I enjoy — but she's too new for that. "So, do you trust me?"

"I mean, I barely know you enough to—"

"It's a simple question, sub," I cut her off, hard. "You either do or you don't."

She's still got her head bent, her gaze on my shoes, and she probably doesn't understand the importance of this question, not really, but she will soon enough.

"What happens if I don't?" she asks breathlessly.

"Nothing except you walking right out that door."

"But how can I answer when—"

Gripping her ponytail tightly, I jerk her head back and I don't bother to be gentle, because I am not gentle. Then I take her sharp chin in my other hand, gripping it so she has no choice but to look straight up at me. Her face is flushed, making her eyes look like quicksilver, and her mouth is a perfect O of surprise. "Yes or no," I demand. "And don't fucking lie. I'll know."

Her gaze clings to mine and I can see the shock there, and it satisfies me. I love that shock in a sub. When they think they have me all figured out and I prove to them how wrong they are. It's exactly the kind of mind game I like to play and the heat inside me intensifies. I've rattled her and she deserves to be rattled, coming in here and thinking she can demand things of me.

I tighten my grip on her, letting her feel my strength. Letting her know who's in charge. "Well? Answer me, sub."

"Y-yes," she stutters in a rush of breath.

Good. There's some steel in her. I like that.

"Third question," I say. "Do you consent to me taking charge of you?"

She's breathing very fast now, reality closing in on her. "I...I...Y-yes."

I grip her chin tighter. "Then here's how this is going to work. I'm going to give you a taste of what it feels like to be my sub, but only a taste, Odette. I'm not going to fuck you or do anything else with you, understand?"

Her brow creases and she opens her mouth to say something, but I put my thumb over her lips, silencing her. She blinks, her body tensing, and I say, iron in my voice. "Don't even think about it. I'm the one in charge now and I'm the one who makes the decisions. Not you."

Wariness enters her gaze and it's about fucking time.

"This will not be easy for you," I go on, so she knows this before we begin. "And you will not like what I'm going to ask you to do. But I don't care if it's difficult or you don't like it. All I care about is that you do it. That's why trust is important, Odette. Being my sub means total and complete obedience to my will."

Her wariness has given way to uncertainty as the reality of what she's asked for slowly penetrates, an awareness of what submission truly means.

"You can pull out." I keep my thumb where it is, pressed against the softness of her mouth. "It's not too late. But understand that if you do, this opportunity won't come again. At least not with me it won't."

She blinks, uncertainty and desire warring in her eyes, and I realize that I haven't seen that look in a sub for a long time. I'd forgotten how much I liked it. When the sub is unsure, caught between her body and her mind. There's a tension there that's addictive, erotic, and fun as hell to play with.

"Well?" I demand. "You want to leave?"

Her muscles are tense and there's doubt in her eyes. She's still not sure. Yet despite that, she slowly shakes her head.

So, the colorless waif has yet more steel. Intriguing, I can't deny it. And surprising. I didn't think she had it in her.

I keep a good grip on her, keep her gaze pinned to mine. "Then here are my rules. You will give me your complete obedience and you will not argue. Your safe word is *red*. If you use your safe word in attempt to control me, I will stop and you will go home." I pause, then add. "For example, that little trick you just pulled by going down on your knees and saying please in an attempt to manipulate me is what's called topping from the bottom and I will not have it. Is that understood?"

Her throat moves as she swallows, the doubt shifting in her eyes. But again, she nods.

I keep holding her for a moment, studying her face. Shit's getting real for her now as she realizes this is not the fun idea she found out about after a couple of internet searches. But she won't understand what she's truly committing herself to, not yet.

I release her, then rise to my full height, still holding her gaze and keeping her trapped by it. Making sure she has nowhere else to look but at me. "You are going to make yourself come," I order her. "And I am going to watch."

5

Odette

My heart is rabbiting about in my chest and I'm finding it difficult to breathe. I don't know whether it's because my second thoughts have grabbed me by the throat and are now choking me, or whether it's him.

I don't know what I thought being his submissive would be like, or what he'd be like as a Dom, but it wasn't this. Maybe subconsciously I expected him to be a harder, older version of his son. Except there's nothing of Lucas in his blue stare. While Lucas's questions made me overthink everything, I knew he was asking because he was trying to make me comfortable. But there's no concern for my comfort in Mr. Fairfax's eyes. I'm prey and now he has me in his sights, he's not going to let me escape.

I couldn't believe it when he first touched my hair. A

delicious shiver of anticipation had gone right through me at the brush of his fingers. I'd felt a little smug, too, that going down on my knees the way I'd read about had worked. But the moment he took my chin in his hand, forcing me to look at him as he laid down the law, his voice breaking over me like an iron rod over my back, all my smugness vanished. I knew I'd made a mistake.

I had a couple of boyfriends before Lucas and the sex with them was fine. Pleasant, but nothing particularly memorable. Lucas is good in bed, but with him I always felt as if it was the sex itself that was the important bit, not me. Even after the attack, I felt as if his kindness and considerateness were because that's what he thought was expected of him and not because he actually wanted to be kind and considerate.

Luc certainly never looked at me the way Mr. Fairfax is looking at me, with a laser-sharp intensity backed by the iron and steel of his will. It's a force, that will—almost palpable, pressing down on me hard, and a part of me wants to bend beneath it. That part frightens me. It reminds me of when I was jumped outside the bar, how I froze like a deer in the headlights of a car. Of how I didn't fight, didn't scream, didn't do anything at all. It was as if it was happening to someone else and I was just an observer, watching from outside my body as I was punched in the face, pressed up against a wall, his hands tearing at my dress.

I was weak in that moment, powerless, and that same sense of powerlessness creeps through me now and I don't know why. I know he won't hurt me, not like my attacker did, but this isn't what I thought I'd be getting myself into and I'm frightened. Yet what's more disturbing is that there's a pressure between my legs, an ache, as if my body likes this and wants this and I don't understand that at all.

"Well?" he demands in that voice that leaves no room for argument or protest, only obedience. "You heard me, sub. Do as you're told."

My mouth is dry and my brain is whirling frantically. "I...I..." I stutter, struggling to think.

Abruptly he reaches down and this time his fingers burrow into my hair beneath my hair elastic to grip it. I gasp because it hurts and then I gasp again as he yanks me roughly upright on my knees, pinpricks of pain erupting all over my scalp.

"I gave you an order, sub," he says, his fist clenched tight in my hair.

Tears start in my eyes. I've never been handled this way before. The only time I was had been when I was attacked, and now it feels as if Mr. Fairfax is doing the same things to me and I can't deal.

He yanks my head back again, so I'm forced to look up at him once more, the intensity of his blue gaze difficult to hold. It makes me feel so vulnerable to be looked at this way, as if he can see all my weaknesses, all my flaws, and I don't want him to see them. I don't want him to look at me that way.

"I told you this wouldn't be easy." He's studying me like a scientist studies an animal he's dissecting. Clinical, analytical. "There's a reason I said no to you, but you insisted. And you forced my hand." His fingers work in my hair, burrowing deeper, curling into a fist and my vision wavers, my eyes full of hurt tears. "But if you don't like it, you can use your safe word. I'll stop and you can go."

My throat aches, my heartbeat like thunder in my head. I can feel yet more tears gather, because his grip hurts and a weird toxic mix of emotion is churning inside me. Fear. Anger. Shock. And perhaps the weirdest of all, desire. And I still don't understand why.

I could say my safe word and get out of here, and part of me really wants to.

He wants you to, too.

It's true, I think, as I'm held captive by his blue stare. He wants me to use it. He expects me to use it. He thinks I can't do this, that I can't handle him.

He's right. You can't.

Something in me hardens unexpectedly. Because no, fuck that. Yes, this is all a shock to the system, but it is something I asked for. Something I wanted. Something I actually insisted on, and sure, I could say *red*. I could turn around and walk away, but where would that leave me? And what would he think of me? I don't know why I care about his opinion, but I can't bear him thinking me a coward. He's so strong, so forceful, and I want to be equal to it. I don't want to be weak.

So I blink my tears away, press my lips together, and shake my head once.

Something flickers in his eyes and it looks like surprise, and the hard part of me, the stubborn part, is abruptly, fiercely glad. He wasn't expecting that, was he? Good. I may be much younger than he is, but that doesn't mean he knows everything, or everything about me.

The surprise vanishes from his eyes, but his grip on my hair doesn't lessen. His face is impassive, his stare relentless. "I won't ask again," he says.

And he won't, that's clear. If I don't do this, he'll let me go and walk out, and that will be it. I won't get a chance to prove myself to anyone, let alone him.

So I swallow and lift a shaking hand, reaching down

over my dress and down between my thighs. His fist tightens in my hair, giving me a hard shake, making me gasp aloud. Yet more tears of pain start in my eyes. "No." His voice is hard, implacable. "Not like that." Before I can take another breath, keeping a firm hold of me, he bends, takes a fistful of my dress, and yanks it up over my hips. "I want to see it, sub," he growls. "I want to see your fingers in your cunt."

The word *cunt* sends a hot shock through me. It's not as if I haven't heard it before, but hearing *him* say it is a whole different thing. The sound of that hard 'c' makes my face flame, yet the pressure between my thighs is increasing. Lucas doesn't do dirty talk, and I'm not used to it, but it's clear my body likes it. My body likes his orders, too, no matter the pain or the fear, and it wants more.

He's looking straight into my eyes and seeing my every thought, knowing I'm finding this difficult and that it's not what I expected. Except there is no *I told you so* in his gaze. It's detached, neutral, passing no judgement, yet the sheer relentlessness of it makes me want to hide.

I can hear how fast I'm breathing, panting almost, and it's not going to work. I won't come with him holding my hair like that, so I force out, "It hurts."

"I know." He makes no move to release me. "I don't care."

I take another panicked breath. "B-but I won't be able to come."

"Yes, you will." He says it as if it's a foregone conclusion. "You will because I told you to."

Yet I'm consumed by the fear that I won't, no matter what he says. That what he's doing is too frightening, too painful and not sexy, and I just won't be able to. I realize that I can't bear the thought. I can't bear the thought that what I'm doing now has just been an awful, terrible mistake. I'm so stupid, so naive. Thinking I could do this, deal with him, and I can't. I'm not brave enough.

My tears overflow and I feel them running down my cheeks, and I don't know why I'm crying. I don't know why this matters so much to me, but it does, and now I can't stop.

Mr. Fairfax watches impassively. "Cry all you want," he says. "It won't make any difference."

I give a little sob. "I…c-can't."

"What did I say about trust?" His gaze doesn't waver from my face. "If I say that you'll come, then you will. Don't second guess and don't think. All you need to do is what I told you."

Say the word. Say red.

That would be so easy, but he told me submission would be hard. I just didn't realize exactly how hard. He told me to trust him, yet that's so difficult to do. My tears mean nothing to him, I can see that, and the fact that his grip hurts means nothing too. Lucas would have comforted me, would have instantly stopped doing anything that would have hurt me.

You didn't want him to be careful with you though. You were tired of that.

It's true. I was. But I wasn't prepared for the harsh reality.

"Give up then," Mr. Fairfax says, his voice dripping with disdain. "I told you that you weren't ready."

I swallow, doing my best to hold his gaze, and that's when I see it. Beyond the impassive wall of his blue stare, a spark of challenge glitters. *Do this,* he is saying. *Do this, I dare you.* And I shiver as something in me rises, punching through my fear, wanting to meet that challenge. A thread of anger, of determination.

So despite my fear and my doubts, I lower my shaking hands to the waistband of my silky, purple panties and I shove them down to my thighs, holding his stare all the while.

I expect him to look down at my pussy, but he doesn't, and somehow that makes it even more difficult. Yet also inexplicably, intensely erotic. He's looking at *me*, not my body, and something in me likes that a lot. It wants to show him that I *can* do this, that I'm *not* a coward, so even though tears are still rolling down my face, I slide my hand down between my thighs. I'm surprised by how wet I am, despite my roiling emotions, and quite frankly it's embarrassing how much my body has disagreed with my head.

Again though, he doesn't look down. "Eyes on me, sub," he orders. "Do *not* look away."

I'm shaking as I stroke my reluctant fingers over my clit, and a gasp escapes me. I'm shocked by how sharp the pleasure is and how it seems to be intensified by his fierce blue stare.

He doesn't speak, noting every little change in my expression, every little flicker of helpless pleasure, studying me with intensity and deliberateness. I can't hide anything from him, not a single thing, and I can't stop trembling as my fingers move over my clit, stroking harder, faster. And I know he's right all of a sudden. I *will* come and I'm going to come hard and I'm almost there—

He reaches out and jerks my hand away.

"No!" I cry out before I can think because fuck, I was so nearly *there*. My orgasms sometimes take ages, but I was about to come so fast, and I can't believe he stopped me. I try to pull my hand from his grip, but it's like trying to get rid of an iron shackle. "Don't," I gasp, promptly forgetting everything he told me about obedience. "Please don't. You told me to make myself come, you told—"

"And now I've changed my mind." His voice is flat, his gaze unwavering.

I'm so turned on I'm in literal pain and I still can't believe he stopped me. "Why?" I demand. "Why did you—"

He doesn't let go of my wrist. "Because I did."

"But I—"

"I don't explain myself to subs," he interrupts, steel in his voice.

I start crying again, I can't help it, silent tears rolling down my face, the pain of thwarted desire throbbing between my legs.

He continues to ignore my tears. "Pull you panties up. You may stand."

I don't want to. I'm so angry that I don't want to do a thing he says. And yet clumsily and with shaking hands, I yank my panties up—shoving my stupid dress down, then getting to my feet. My knees are weak, I'm still so close to orgasm I want to scream, and I don't know why I'm still crying.

He gazes at me without any discernible expression, his blue eyes enigmatic, and lets the silence sit there for far longer than I want it to. Then he says, "That was fifteen minutes. Time for you to leave."

I heave in a shaky breath, anger at him and at my own stupid weakness rising and rising. Furiously, I swipe at my wet cheeks. "You can't do that," I say thickly. "You can't say those things to me and—"

"I gave you a taste of what submission feels like." He cuts me off, his voice iron and steel. "If you want to find out more, there are plenty of Dominants on the app to choose from."

Fury burns hot inside me, in fact, I can't remember the last time I was so angry. In fact, I'm so furious I'm crying again, and I'm tempted to finish myself off in front of him anyway, just to spite him. I lower my hand but he says, "Don't you fucking dare."

And much to my intense rage, I obey. His hard blue stare is too much, and I'm just not brave enough.

"Fine," I say furiously. "Fuck you then."

Then I grab my purse and I leave.

6

Gideon

I'm sitting in my office in the Fairfax building, in downtown Manhattan, with Lucas sitting in the chair on the other side of my desk. My son wanted to *talk* and so here he is, in my office, talking. And fuck, it's all the kids want to do these days, endless talking about their lives and *processing* of their feelings, and I don't have the patience for it. But he's my son and I haven't been there in the past for him, so here I am, listening.

Or rather, I'm pretending to listen, because my brain won't stop thinking about something else.

It's been three days since Odette stormed out of my hotel room, which usually means out of sight, out of mind, but she is not out of my mind. She's been occupying it ever since that night and it's getting really fucking annoying.

I don't know why I can't stop thinking about that night.

Can't stop thinking of her, on her knees, her fingers stroking her exceptionally pretty and very wet pussy. The flush in her cheeks, the darkness of her silvery eyes, the redness of her mouth. The intense fight she had with herself about obeying my commands and how she didn't want to do it. The tears rolling down her cheeks, the battle she had with not wanting to trust me, and yet wanting to at the same time.

The war a sub has between her fears and her desires is such a fucking aphrodisiac to me, and I can't say I wasn't... unaffected. In fact, that was the reason I had to get her out of there, because I *was* affected and I didn't like it. Getting hard is one thing, that's easily solved, but the Dominant in me was hungry for her in a way that went beyond simple release. I was surprised by her strength, and wanted to explore it. Test it. Show her how that strength could give her the most intense pleasure. And I wanted to find out what else was surprising about her, which was dangerous.

But you're bored. You like surprises.

Yes, both of those things are true. Except I don't want to get interested in a sub, especially not after a scene is over. What happens in the playroom stays in the fucking playroom, and there's no thinking about it later. At least, I never have before and so I can't fathom why the fuck I'm doing it now.

"So," Lucas says, leaning back in his chair and putting one foot on the opposite knee. "What would you say to me dropping out of Yale?"

I force my attention away from Odette and bring it back to my son. He's a cocky little prick, but then I was the same when I was his age. Young, rich, good-looking, with the world mine for the taking. To be fair though, I was never rich. I had nothing but ambition and a steely desire to prove my asshole parents wrong, and it's that which got me where I am today.

I stare at him from the other side of my desk. He's studying economics with a view to taking over the business from me eventually, but being a college dropout does not feature in that plan.

I don't react, though. I simply keep staring at him. "Why?"

"The truth?" He stares back at me with the same intensity, which naturally he got from me. "I'm bored. I need to get out of here, out of the country, and go and be in a different place for a while."

He's also inherited my stubbornness and while he's never been without ambition, this was not what I was expecting.

"Lucas," I begin.

"I'm going to put my studies on hold," he says before I can go on. "But I need some time out."

I raise a brow. "Are you asking for my permission?"

"No." He lifts his chin, already being defiant, because he knows the answer to that. "This is purely for information's sake."

I have to hand it to him. Once he's decided something, he does it, no fucking around. I wonder if this has something to do with the fallout of his mother's death and not for the first time, I regret not being there for him. Maintaining a good relationship with someone is like putting money in the bank. There's a certain level of funds there, so that when withdrawals occur, you have enough money left to keep the account open. But I don't have enough money in the bank with Lucas and we both know it.

"It's not what we agreed when you said you wanted to go to Yale," I say. "You wanted to finish your degree before you did anything else."

"Yeah, I know," he says, still defiant. "But I changed my mind."

He does not elaborate, but something makes me ask, "And Odette? What about her? Is she going with you?"

His gaze flickers and he looks away. Every muscle in my body tenses. She can't have told him what happened between her and me, because I'm pretty sure he wouldn't currently be sitting here talking to me if she had. But who knows? She was very angry when I kicked her out, and she had every right to be. I wouldn't have done things differently, though. Fifteen minutes was enough to tell me that despite the unexpected glimpse of steel in her, she still wouldn't be able to handle anything more. Not considering how she was crying after five.

"That's not a thing anymore," Lucas says, picking at the fabric on the arm of his chair. "It's over."

I'm sure that's not satisfaction rising in me. It can't be, because why? I told her to go and find herself another Master, that I wasn't available, end of story. I'm certainly not chasing her now she's not with my son. I'm not that fucking desperate.

"Oh?" I ask, making sure to mask the curiosity in my voice. "Did you finally let her off the hook?"

"No." Lucas jerks at the threads on the chair arm. "She... dumped me."

I blink, aware of deep surprise. She told me that night that she wanted to explore her sexuality for Lucas's sake, so what made her change her mind? Was it me? Was it what we did?

"What happened?" This time I can't quite disguise the note of demand in my voice.

But Lucas doesn't pick up on it — thank God for the self-centeredness of young people. "Oh, she said it wasn't working between us and that she thought it was better if we had some time apart." He finally looks up from the chair arm. "It's fine. We were kind of over each other anyway. She's clingy and super anxious, and I know that's because of the attack, but—"

"What attack?" I interrupt sharply as everything draws tight inside me.

Luc sighs. "Oh, it was a year ago. She was jumped by some asshole outside a bar and got hurt. She dropped out of college because of it."

I struggle to keep my expression neutral as a flare of instinctive and protective anger licks up inside me. Generalized anger at cowards who think hurting women makes them feel powerful is one thing, but this sharp needle of fury is quite another. It feels almost personal, though there is no reason for it to be. Apart from that one hour in my hotel room, I haven't spoken more than a few words to her and certainly never spent time with her, so I don't know why I feel this intensely about it.

Lucas is frowning at me and I realize that maybe I haven't managed to hide my feelings as well as I should. "That's unfortunate," I say coolly. "Clearly security needs to do a better job."

"Yeah, well, she was in a bad way for a while and I didn't want to make things worse by dumping her in the middle of it."

"You weren't doing her a favor," I can't help but say. "Persisting with something that doesn't work only makes things worse in the long run. You should have been up front with her about it, had the difficult conversation. She let you off the hook."

Lucas stares at me. "Coming from you, that's rich. You're the king of avoiding difficult conversations."

Fuck. Little shit isn't wrong. Nothing like your children to find your weak points to slide the knife in.

"You want to have it now, then?" I say, because I can't let that go unchallenged. "I've got nothing on my schedule. I'm free all afternoon."

Lucas snorts and pushes himself from the chair. "Fuck, no. The moment when we could have had that conversation was years ago and you fucking missed it." He starts towards the doors.

"Luc." I don't know why I want him to stop, turn around, and sit down again. Not when I have no idea what to say to him. Nevertheless, I do.

He stops and glances back at me. "Yeah, what?"

But I still have no idea what to say and in the end I say nothing.

"Thought so," Lucas says, scathingly, and walks out.

Fuck. Another excellent interaction with my son.

I shove my chair back and stalk over to the windows, consumed with the need to move. I'm pissed at myself. All the years in business gave me an extremely low bullshit threshold and after Gabrielle's death that threshold only got lower. I always mean what I say and I never second-guess myself, and the only regrets I have are around Lucas and Gabrielle, so talking to my son should not be so difficult. Yet it is.

As I stare moodily over New York City's skyline, I feel my phone vibrate in my pocket. I pull it out and look down at the screen. It's a notification from The Club app that I have a new message.

My anger coils and tightens like a snake unable to find a target, and I know that when I'm feeling like this, I need to feed the beast. I need to setup another playdate with a pretty little sub. Domination is simple when everyone knows the rules and there is no need to think of anything else. There is only the sub and their obedience. Their pleasure. Taking control of a sub is a rush I've never found anywhere else. It centers me completely, puts me straight in the moment, and reminds me that control is everything. Control over one's body and one's emotions. It's meditative sometimes, too, and when you can reduce a sub to a screaming, crying mess, you know you've done your job well.

Fuck, I need this.

I open the app and scroll to my messages. There are a few from subs looking to find a new Master, but that's not me, so I ignore those ones. A couple from subs I'm familiar with, who want a playdate, and yet even as I'm thinking about responding, I'm ambivalent. I know them already and they know me, and once you're a known quantity, can there ever be surprises? I know their boundaries and they know mine and the tension of uncertainty, of trepidation, that can make a scene so fucking hot, is lost.

I scroll past them, dissatisfied, and just then a new message arrives and instantly every muscle in my body tenses.

It's from Artemis.

What the fuck? I told her she wasn't ready, that she needed to find someone else, so why the hell is she pushing? I don't do brats.

My thumb hovers over the message, ready to delete it without even opening it, yet I find myself hitting open instead. It's a photo. She's on her knees, entirely naked. Her white-blonde hair cascades down around her shoulders, and far from being sleek like I'd imagined from her ponytail, it's curly. She's staring into the camera, her gray eyes steady. Her skin is pale, the nipples of her small breasts a delicate pink, and she has her hands on her knees, palms up, like an obedient sub should.

Above the photo are the words: *I'm ready, Sir.*

And all the blood in my body rushes down to my groin, my cock getting hard. The Dominant in me stirs restlessly, remembering that night and the intensity of her reaction to me. Her tears and her arousal, our battle of wills. The surprise and satisfaction I felt when she jerked her panties down and touched herself, even though she didn't want to. The silvery glitter of fury in her eyes as I told her to leave...

Yes, she's ready. She was ready back in that hotel room, and you knew it the moment she put her fingers on her pussy.

I grit my teeth, trying to force the desire down, deny those thoughts. She was crying and didn't want to do what I told her to, so of course she wasn't ready.

You've pushed other subs to that place before. It's not about her readiness. It's about yours.

I scrub a hand across my face, wanting to reject that idea yet not being able to. A weeping, emotional sub isn't unusual for me, but being affected by one certainly is. That hasn't happened to me before, and I can't think why it did with Odette.

Was it only the lure of the forbidden? Her being Lucas's girlfriend? Or was it something else?

Perhaps you should find out?

It's impossible, of course. That would mean going back on what I told her, that she should find another Dominant. It also means allowing myself to be manipulated by that pretty photo.

She needs another lesson.

Fuck's sake. She really does, but I don't teach new subs and I don't train them, no matter how badly they want to be taught or trained.

Christ, did she dump Lucas so she could message me? It that why she's *ready?* Not that it matters. She *was* his girlfriend and she's so much younger than I am, and then there's the attack that Lucas mentioned...

So many reasons why I should delete her message.

Yet I don't. I stand by the windows, looking down at the photo, my cock hard while my Dominant side, impatient with my scruples, wants to set up the playdate already.

Are they scruples? Or are they lies?

I don't want to think about it, because deep down I know the truth. They *are* lies. If I'd truly not wanted her, I'd have deleted her message and set up a playdate with one of the other subs. I wouldn't be staring down at this photo of a lovely naked woman, thinking how good her tits would look with a pair of jeweled nipple clamps.

It's wrong, especially considering the attack that Luc told me about. The very last thing she should want after that is a man being hard with her. Then again...I was hard with her three nights ago and even though she flinched, she didn't back out. There was steel in her. And it's not unprecedented for some subs to work through violence issues with a Dom. If that's what she's doing, she really needs to be with someone who knows how to assist with that...

Christ, perhaps it's a lie I'm telling myself to make it okay, but I can't let it go. There are good Dominants in The Club. They wouldn't be there if they weren't good— yet I still don't like the idea of her going to someone else, someone who might not know what happened to her.

The nagging tightness in my groin is undeniable and I reach down to adjust myself. Fuck's sake. It's ridiculous to be hard for a woman who has no idea what she wants or what she's getting into, and yet I am. So maybe that's why I make my decision.

One night. One night only. That's all she needs and that's certainly all I need.

I hit reply and send her a message.

7

Odette

I'm shaking as the message appears in my inbox on The Club app and I have to sit down on my ratty old couch. I can't believe he replied, and so quickly, because I was certain he wouldn't. Especially after what he told me about topping from the bottom. That's kind of what I was doing sending him that photo of me, so he'd be well within his rights to ignore me or issue a slap down. But he didn't and it's not a slap down. The message is a time, date, and an address, and then *More instructions to follow*.

I sit there, staring down at my phone, almost hyperventilating.

The night he sent me away, I went home nearly weeping with fury as thwarted desire coursed through me. I was severely tempted to finish myself off just to spite him, but in the end I didn't. It felt like giving in or giving him power that I didn't want him to have. Instead, I angrily cleaned my cramped apartment, then took a cold shower and went to bed.

Of course, I dreamed about him, which I was furious about. I didn't want to dream of him. I didn't want to think of him at all, and yet that's all I found myself doing. He even invaded my thoughts at work and I nearly spilled hot coffee on someone.

I tried to push him aside. I shoved him and his fierce blue stare to the back of my mind and tried to go about my life as a semi-normal person. But he just wouldn't leave. That night and he had gotten into my head and I couldn't get him out again.

After the attack my life had gotten so small. I quit college, found the world's tiniest apartment and I stayed in it. I didn't go out. I had to get a job at a place near where I lived because I didn't want to have to take the subway. Too many people, too many strangers. I read books and watched TV and ate takeout and didn't go anywhere or do anything. I'd accepted that's what my life was now, and it was kind of... gray. Like I've been sleeping, the world shrouded in cotton balls, muffling sounds and muting feelings.

But that night with Mr. Fairfax had changed me. He injected color into all that gray, gave me the briefest taste of something that frightened the shit out of me, and turned me on so intensely I could hardly stand it before sending me off into a wild rage. He'd ripped all those cotton balls away. He'd stripped me of a protective shell I hadn't even known I'd developed, then dumped me, naked and vulnerable, right in the middle of something so raw and intense I'd been overwhelmed.

I'm awake now. I feel strange and new and weirdly alive, and I want more.

I'd truly thought, before that night, that I'd go back to

Hard Discipline

Lucas armed with my newfound knowledge about myself. That I'd tell him what I wanted, and he'd give it to me, and our relationship would be great.

Except, after that encounter with Mr. Fairfax, I knew I'd been lying to myself. That it wasn't Lucas I wanted. That the reason our relationship was bad wasn't about the sex, it was that we were tired of each other. He was only with me because of the attack and I was only with him because.... Well, he was familiar and he was nice to me. Which was a great start to a relationship, but it can't be the whole of it. So I had to let him go, set him free, because it was his father I wanted.

Once I'd done that, it took me another day to muster up the courage to message Mr. Fairfax on the app. I spent all morning checking out all the other Masters at The Club, just so I could say that I had, but even as I scrolled through their bios, I knew I wasn't going message them. It would always be Master Six for me. I wasn't sure what to say in my message or what would change his mind about me, but in the end I went with a nude, because my body was all I had to offer him.

So now I'm staring at his message, half of me ecstatic that he replied so quickly and half of me terrified of what I've gotten myself into. This message clearly is about a meeting, especially with the *more instructions to follow* thing.

I swallow as the words on the screen blur and then spring into focus again. He wants to do this, with me, but why did he change his mind? Is it because he must know by now that I've dumped Lucas? Or was it the pic?

My thoughts spiral around and around, adrenaline coursing through me. Do I respond? Is he expecting me to? He must, surely, because he'll want to know that the dates and times are good for me. Shall I check my diary? That date is a week away, but I know there's no need to cheek my stupid diary, because there's nothing in there.

Still feeling as if I'm having a weird, out-of-body experience, I type *Okay* as a reply and then hit send before the second-thoughts can get to me.

The week passes both incredibly fast and with aching slowness, and I can't concentrate on anything. Lucas texts me to say he's dropping out of Yale and going overseas and I feel happy for him. He probably needs that. But of course my mind goes immediately to Mr. Fairfax and what he thinks about that, because I know Lucas said his father wanted him finish his degree before he did anything else. Maybe I can ask him about that when I see him?

To fill my time, I do endless internet searches about BDSM, familiarizing myself with terms and equipment and toys. It scares me, not going to lie, but it also makes me squirm in my chair at the thought of Mr. Fairfax using some of those toys and equipment on me. I don't understand why I'm petrified, yet also turned on at the same time. It makes no sense.

To give myself a break from that, I also do searches on Mr. Gideon Fairfax and his billion-dollar company, scrolling through photos of him at various high-society galas and fundraisers, as well as reading all the gossip column inches I can find.

I knew he lost his wife ten years ago and the rumors are that he mourns her still. Lucas didn't mention much about his parents' relationship, only that when his mom died, things with his father began to fall apart— so maybe it's true that Mr. Fairfax is grieving. Grieving so much he lost touch with his son.

It makes my heart ache for him, which is strange because it's not as if I know him that well or anything. In fact, given how hard he was with me that night we had our encounter, I shouldn't feel anything for him but rage. And that's there, sure, but also...something more. The news articles give a tantalizing glimpse of the man behind that hard blue stare, a man who felt deeply enough about someone that he hasn't had a girlfriend since — at least if those gossip columns are true.

The morning of our date finally comes and true to his word, he sends me some instructions that I'm to follow to the letter. A car will arrive to pick me up at 5pm sharp. I can wear anything I like, but not underwear. Red lipstick and high heels are mandatory. My hair is to be loose. He doesn't mention showering or shaving, but I do both anyway, just in case.

I'm a nervous wreck by the time 5pm comes and when I leave my apartment building, I find a fucking limo waiting at the curb. The driver leaps out, asks me for my name, and when I give it he opens the door and ushers me inside like I'm the Queen of England. I sit dry-mouthed on the soft leather seats, my heart doing somersaults in my chest, my stomaching knotting with anxiety.

The driver is quiet as we glide along the streets of Manhattan, and I have to quell the urge to chatter nervously to fill the silence. I have no idea where we're going, having promptly forgotten the address he gave me, and I can't sit still. I'm shifting constantly on the seat, hideously aware that I'm not wearing any underwear. The dress I'm wearing is a plain blue one I got on sale from H&M. It's not particularly sexy, but I think it makes my eyes look a little less colorless. I'm very conscious of the soft brush of cotton against my bare skin, especially over my nipples, which have gone all hard and pointy. Embarrassing. I hope the driver doesn't notice.

Eventually, we stop outside one of the newer, towering skyscrapers downtown. The driver lets me out at the front of the building and again I'm feeling self-conscious as the doorman — clearly expecting me — gives me and my nipples an impersonal smile and pulls open the door.

It's definitely not a hotel, which I was expecting, so I don't know quite what to think as I walk into a very nice, surprisingly old school kind of lobby with a beautifully carved wooden reception desk. The man behind the desk indicates an elevator nearby with its doors open. I step inside, look at the buttons, and realize that this elevator is a private one.

Butterflies flutter madly in my stomach as the elevator rises and my palms are sweaty while my brain is chasing itself around in circles. What is this place? Do I want to be here? And do I *really* want to try this with him again? Or is this all just a terrible mistake?

That night in the hotel with him replays endlessly in my head and how the reality of it was like a slap in the face. How his hand in my hair was rough and it hurt, and how I cried. And also — I couldn't forget this if I tried — how fast the pleasure had me in its grip.

My second-thoughts constrict around me. I'm not doing this with just anyone, but *him*. Hard, implacable, ruthless. Taller, stronger, older, more experienced. Just...so much *more* than I am. It's a frightening thought, though I'm not sure why. Perhaps it's the power differential, or perhaps not. Perhaps I'm more of a coward than I think I am.

The elevator finally stops and I take a breath. It's feels a bit like *deja vu* from the previous week, me coming up in an elevator to his hotel suite— except this isn't a hotel. The lobby made it seem as if this is an apartment building, which is weird, because surely he can't be inviting me into his own home?

The doors open and I realize they open directly into an apartment, because right in front of me is a short hallway and through an open double doorway I can see a massive open space. Huge windows, high ceilings, thick charcoal carpet. There are soft-looking modular couches in a dark, dusty purple, clearly taking center stage because everything else is shades of black and gray.

Holy shit. *Is* this his place?

I walk into the room and then stand there, staring around open-mouthed. The decor is the kind of luxury that doesn't need to shout, with lots of textures and different materials. Dark wood, charcoal wool, a kind of pewter color on the walls. It's got a cozy atmosphere like it's a place to curl up in. A place to sit on that ridiculously comfortable looking couch with a mug of hot chocolate and book while rain strikes against the glass.

"Good," a deep voice says from behind me. "You wore the heels."

I turn, and my mouth dries, and all of a sudden I remember why I'm doing this. Why I couldn't be with anyone else. And why he makes me so nervous. I'm afraid of him, yet I'm also not afraid him, which doesn't make sense, yet it's true all the same.

Gideon Fairfax is standing there with his arms folded across his broad chest. He's wearing similar clothes to those he wore last week, perfectly tailored pants of dark gray wool, though this time his shirt is blue. It's the same color as his eyes. Those eyes are enigmatic, the expression on his brutally handsome face giving nothing away. But that will of his, that aura of forceful command, fills the room like a storm front, almost suffocating me.

"A-a-and the lipstick," I force out, stuttering like an idiot, my nervous smile more a grimace than anything else.

He does not smile back. "First. A little housekeeping. Did you read my bio on the app?"

I blink. Bio? App? Fuck, I need to get my head in the game, not let his presence stupefy me like this. I struggle to think of what to say, because while I looked at the other Doms' bios, I didn't look at his. I mean, the first time I found him on the app I did, but I didn't know what any of the terms meant. Also, I was also too anxious to pay attention, so I ended up skimming it. "Umm," I begin, wishing I'd given the thing at least another glance before coming here.

"So, you didn't," he goes on, correctly reading my expression. "That's fine, I don't give a fuck if you read it or not, that'll be on you. Because you'll have to bear the consequences."

"Fuck around and find out?" I ask, like a half-wit.

"Quite literally, I'm afraid." He still isn't smiling. Maybe Doms don't smile. "So, a quick summary about me as a Master. I'm hardline with an emphasis on discipline. I'm into orgasm denial and edging, and I like to test the boundaries of what a sub can bear. I have it down to a fine art and believe me, I can make you scream and cry and plead for release, but I'll only give it to you if I think you've earned it." He pauses a moment, then adds. "But I'm not going to tell you what you have to do to earn it. That's something you'll have to figure out on your own. It probably also goes without saying that I like mind games."

I don't know what I was expecting, but it's not for him to get straight to business within seconds of me walking into the room. No *hi, how are you?* or *how was your day?* or *nice to see you.* Not even an ice-breaker offer of a drink.

My heartbeat thunders in my head, my mouth dry as I

go over what he said. It doesn't sound too bad, except for the screaming and crying bit. Then again, he had me crying and partly screaming last week when he stopped me from climaxing, so maybe I can deal. And as for the hardline business, well, yeah, duh, at least I know that already.

"Okay," I say, trying to not to stutter this time as I shove the fears and doubts away.

"Your safe word will be *red,*" he says. "And as I said last week, be careful how you use it. If you say it to control me, that will be the end of the evening. If you don't say it when you should, that will also be the end of the evening. If you say it because you need a break, I'll stop what I'm doing to allow you to collect yourself."

I nod, my gut full of knots, my palms sweaty.

His blue eyes narrow as he surveys me, but I still can't discern what he's thinking. "Do you have any questions?"

I can only think of one. "Why did you change your mind?"

8

Gideon

Her gray eyes look blue tonight, taking color from the simple cotton dress she's wearing. It looks incongruous with the stripper heels and red lipstick, but not with her hair, worn loose as I directed, a tumble of pale curls.

Good. Obedient.

I find no fault with the way she follows instructions. Still, I can't deny second-guessing my decision to have her come here, where I live. Usually I meet my dates at a hotel because it's impersonal and adds distance, but this is my home and the only person who visits me here is Lucas. Then again, there's a certain ease that comes with having a scene here, mainly due to me having complete control over my environment and also access to all my toys. Having them delivered and picked up from various places is a fucking hassle.

It's better not to think too deeply about that, though, and certainly not when she's asking questions. I allow subs to ask a few things before a scene so they can get fears or doubts out of the way, and if they're honest with me, I'm honest with them. I'm a hardline Dom, but I'm also fair. So even though I don't particularly want to answer this question, especially when I can barely articulate it to myself, I answer, "Your photo was a pretty one. And you dumped my son."

She colors. "I'm sorry about Luc, but—"

"You don't have to explain." I don't want to talk to her about Lucas right now. "It's got nothing to do with me."

"Um, a-actually, it's got everything to do with you." Her voice is husky and I can hear her nerves, but also that note of determination in the words.

She wants you.

It's nothing I didn't already know. She wouldn't have pushed me that night in the hotel room, then sent a follow up message if she didn't. I'm used to women wanting me and I don't say that with arrogance, it's just the truth, so I don't know why the thought of this particular woman wanting me is so...arousing.

It's not her youth — I've been with subs younger than I am as well as subs who are older, and it's not the age of the person or their appearance that matters to me. It's their mind— what drives them, what excites them, and what scares them that interests me.

She's certainly a pretty package, though, and I'm not made of stone. I like naked women as much as the next heterosexual man, but there were elements of her that surprised me that night and it's those elements that are drawing me in right now.

Her obvious nervousness. Her wariness. The way her

eyes are already darkening as they look into mine, a sure sign that she's in a state of arousal. The fact that I made her wait a week so she'd remember what happened between us last time and maybe rethink things if she wanted, yet she still turned up here. She's honest, ending things with Lucas before she messaged me, and even though I didn't give her an easy lesson, she's back and wanting more, and that speaks to a certain courage.

I *do* like a plucky little sub.

"I'm not your boyfriend, Odette," I tell her. "So if that's what you're hoping for, you can forget it."

Her fingers move restlessly on the strap of her purse. "No. I...I didn't mean that. I j-just...." She trails off, her gaze dropping before the force of mine, and that sign of instinctive submission is like a long, slow stroke down the length of my cock.

A silence falls and I let it while she shifts on her feet, so antsy and nervous as the tension pulls tighter and tighter. It's arousing, watching her be so anxious and unsettled, and knowing that it's all because of me.

"It wasn't just about your picture, Odette," I say at last, deciding to give her a little more honesty as a reward for her bravery.

She looks up instantly, silver eyes wide.

"You're a pretty girl, but pretty I can get anywhere," I go on. "That night though, you displayed a certain.... strength. I found it intriguing and decided I wanted to test it over the course of a night. Test it fully."

Her mouth opens then closes, her face flushing. She's pleased with that, which is interesting. Most women prefer compliments on their appearance, not observations about their strength, but she certainly likes it, and, strangely, I find that arousing too. Strange, because while I get off on a sub's pleasure, it's usual direct physical pleasure rather than the pleasure of delivering a compliment. It's good, though. Just another piece of the puzzle I can use to amp up her reactions, later.

"Another thing," I continue, because I need to get this out of the way and it's important that she knows I'm aware of it. Honesty is vital with a new sub and trust is everything, so I won't hide things from her. "Luc told me what happened to you. About how you were attacked."

Her expression freezes and she blinks. "What?"

I don't repeat myself, letting the quiet sit there, studying her as her face loses the frozen look, a sudden storm of emotion blowing across it. Interesting how open she is. Maybe it's youth, or maybe that's who she is, unable to keep from broadcasting every thought in her head. One thing is clear though: she's angry

"He had no right to say anything to you," she says furiously. "It's not his story to tell."

Interesting. Lucas didn't say it was a secret but she's certainly acting as if it was. Why? I get that it must have been traumatic for her, and clearly it's a private matter, but is it really of any consequence if I know? Does it matter to her what I think?

"Nevertheless, he told me," I say calmly.

This time she meets my gaze without any trouble whatsoever and there it is in her eyes, that steel. It's bright and gleaming and I get a sense of its strength. This woman may look fragile and breakable, but she has a backbone of pure iron, and once again I feel it, that kick of raw heat. I want to push her, test her, match my steel with hers and see what happens. Fucking sparks, I can already tell.

"It's behind me," she says, her voice flat. "It was a year ago and I'm over it. I don't want you to see me any differently or treat me any differently, because I'm not a fucking victim, okay?"

No she is not, and that is very clear. Yet she's also afraid that secretly she might be, because what else is behind all that anger but fear? It gives me more context for why she's here and why she wants me in particular. Why my brand of Domination is something she's afraid of and yet yearns for. I'm not the only one who wants to test her; she wants to test herself too. Good. I can do that.

"I will treat you any way I see fit," I point out mildly. "But that is information you should have told me."

Her jaw firms. "Why? It's none of your damn business."

"Everything that goes on in this room is my damn business, and that includes you and your safety. Not being aware of a sub's issues because she's been keeping secrets can be dangerous. Are we clear?"

She stares at me belligerently, still pissed as hell.

I stare back, implacable, unrelenting. "Answer me, sub. If you don't like any of those rules, you know where the door is."

Odette bites her lip and glances down at the carpet. Her jaw is still tight and so is the rest of her body. It looks as if she's bracing herself for another attack. Perhaps I should give her some reassurance, but I am not that kind of man. Besides, the Master in me knows that's not what she needs. What she needs is to be tested, so she can see for herself the strength that I see in her.

So I say nothing, letting her decide what she wants.

A couple of moments pass and then she lets out a breath. "Okay," she mutters, then looks at me again. "Fine."

Again, she's proving her courage, and I find myself pleased that she's decided to stay. The longer she's here the more of her I see and yes, I like what I see. Very much.

For a moment I debate the merits of asking her about the attack so I'm aware of any potential triggers, but that could end up being unhelpful. Especially in cases like this one, where a sub is working through issues she doesn't even know she has and needs to be confronted with her own fears so she can face and overcome them.

In the end though, I say nothing, letting yet more silence fall since silence can be a great tool to mess with a sub's head.

She continues to shift on her feet, clutching at her worn purse of pale leather, still salty as fuck with me judging from the silver flickers of temper in her eyes. "So," she says impatiently, breaking the silence as I knew she would, "What would you like me to—"

"Quiet." I interrupt, command deepening my voice. "You remember what I told you last week? About the rules?"

"Yes."

Her hands are shaking a little and I like that. I like everything about her right now, her anger and uncertainty, her anxiety and her impatience. All emotional cues I can use to make her feel so good, so very, *very* good.

Now. It's time to let the Master out to play.

"Keep your heels on," I order. "But take off the rest of your clothes. Fold them neatly and lay them on the floor next to the couch, along with your purse. Then kneel in front of the windows, facing the room."

She takes a breath and stares at me for a long second as the reality of what she's come here for gradually sinks in, but I hold her gaze, pinning her where she stands. Imposing my will on her through the sheer force of my presence. I can sense how she's trying to hold my gaze, to not look down, but I will not allow it.

The battle of wills lasts only a couple of seconds, but the

thrill of it gets into my blood like a line of the very best coke, and when she eventually drops her gaze, *fuck* it's a rush. I'm getting hard, which is unusual so early into a scene, but that's fine. It's nothing I can't handle.

She puts her purse down next to the couch, then begins to undo her dress. A gentleman would help her with the zipper, but I'm no gentleman, so all I do is watch as she manages to get it down herself. Her hands shake and uncertainty flickers over her face, but the flush that warms her pale cheeks and spreads down her neck beneath the blue cotton betrays her. Even if she's not conscious of it, she likes being watched.

The fabric slides from her shoulders and down, following her slight curves until she's standing naked in a puddle of blue cotton, and she's sexy as fuck, can't deny it. All pale skin, with small, high breasts, pink and pretty nipples, lusciously curved hips, and a bare pussy. I didn't ask her to shave — hair doesn't bother me — but I like it. It means I can see everything.

I continue to stand there, unmoving, watching as she awkwardly folds her clothes up and lays them near the couch like I asked her to. She's incredibly self-conscious, her movements stiff and uncertain, but I don't comment and don't make any attempt to go easy on her. No matter what she said about not wanting to be treated like a victim, she expects me treat her exactly like that and I'm aware of it. I wonder if that's how she's been treated in the rest of her life, with cosseting and coddling, and I wonder if she's tired of it.

I wonder if that's what she's searching for, something different.

Still, I've been looking forward to this, even though I shouldn't. I found myself thinking about it at random points in the day, even in the middle of important meetings. About the best way to discover her vulnerabilities and her desires, about what makes her tick and how to use that to test her, push her, bring her the most pleasure.

It's always about a sub's pleasure, that's always the goal, because if they're not getting off then I'm not getting off and so what would be the point? I'm not hardline out of meanness, or spite, or anger. I'm hardline because I like it and because it's extremely erotic for the subs who want that in a Dom. And part of the fun is planning what to do to a sub, what little mind games to play, what equipment to use, and how best to send them into subspace.

I always anticipate the planning stage, but I hadn't realized how much I was anticipating the thrill of discovery. It's been a while since I've had a brand-new-to-me sub, and I'd forgotten how much I like figuring out their wants and needs. Thinking about the night with Odette has had me distracted for most of the week. I made her wait, of course, because that's part of the game, as was not telling her that she'd be in my apartment. That was another little surprise to put her off-balance.

Slowly, she kneels where I instructed her to, shifting around so the heels of her shoes don't dig into her soft skin. She's a pretty sight kneeling on the dark carpet, all pale and pink, cascades of curly white-blonde hair, and large silver eyes. Her hands are on her knees, palms up, as she stares down at floor.

So far, so perfect.

I walk slowly over to where she's kneeling, gazing down at her. I can see goosebumps rising on her skin and the tips of her pretty tits are hard. Between her thighs, her bare pussy is glistening. Christ, she's wet already and I've barely started. My cock responds predictably, but again, I ignore it. Plenty of time for that later.

I don't speak. I merely stare down at her, drawing out the seconds of silence and keeping her waiting. She doesn't move, but her gaze darts nervously up at me and then away again, and I can hear the quickening of her breathing.

"Are you afraid?" I ask at last.

Her gaze flickers up. "Oh no. I'm actually—"

That's when I lunge, reaching down and grabbing a fistful of her hair, jerking her head back. She gasps aloud, her silver eyes going wide, her body arched back in a bow.

"Do not fucking lie to me." My tone is hard and flat, my gaze a scalpel's blade cutting right through her. "You did that last time, sub. I want the truth. *Now*."

She swallows convulsively, the long pale length of her throat exposed, and her eyes are liquid with sudden tears. My grip is hurting her, but I don't let up. She knows what to say if she doesn't want this.

"I-I-I...." Her breathing is coming in short hard gasps. "I-I mean, y-yes."

"Good," I say, watching her reactions like a hawk. "You should be afraid, because tonight will not be easy for you. Especially if you insist on lying. The truth is vital, sub, and if you do not give it to me, then you can leave."

Her skin is warm beneath my fingertips, and silky soft, and the tarnished silver of her eyes is darkening rapidly. She's still panting in my grip, her pale body bowed, her hard little nipples standing out. "I...I-I won't lie," she gasps out. "I p-p-promise...."

"No," I instruct. 'You say, 'I promise, *Master*'."

9

Odette

I'm trembling all over, deafened by the sound of my own heartbeat. Mr. Fairfax has his fingers buried in my hair, my head pulled so far back it's painful. His burning blue eyes take up all my vision, searing my soul, and I'm so aware of him—of how he's bent over me, of his sheer physical strength and power. He could break me in two if he wanted to, but he won't, and some subconscious part of me knows that. That power is under his tight control, and all I can think about is how during the attack, the man who hurt me wasn't controlled in the slightest and how that was the scariest part. He was furious, though I don't know what at, calling me vicious names and punching me, shoving me roughly. It was like being at the mercy of a rabid dog.

But though Mr. Fairfax is being rough with me, there is

no anger in his eyes. He's fierce, but it's a controlled ferocity, and I don't know why that's so fucking hot, but it is.

I thought he might be too careful with me when he mentioned knowing about the attack, and I was furious that Lucas told him. I didn't want him to know, because there are so many things about it that I just don't want to revisit, still less recount to this powerful, strong man. Still, when he did mention it, he was very matter-of-fact and there was no hint of judgment in his eyes, so that was something. I suppose it's true that he should know what happened to me in case anything triggers me, but that didn't mean I wanted him going easy on me.

Part of me is regretting that now, though, as he holds me fast in an iron grip. It's brutal but it's a controlled brutality and while the regrets churn away, other parts of me glory in the roughness of his handling. As if I can take it. As if I'm strong.

I gasp aloud as his grip tightens, reminding me that he needs an answer and so I force out the words, my voice hoarse and shaken, "Y-yes, I p-promise, M-Master."

He doesn't release me — if anything his grip tightens — and it hurts. It makes my eyes water, sends prickles of pain all over my scalp. But there's something about the pain, about the way he's standing over me, about my own nakedness while he's fully clothed, that intensifies the vicious throb between my legs in a way I don't quite understand.

Undressing before him, folding my clothes and putting them next to the couch, had been so incredibly awkward and yet it had also been so hot. Especially with him watching my every move, knowing he could see every part of my body. I found myself wanting to know if he thought I was pretty, or sexy, or whether any part of my body appealed to him. But I could barely bring myself to meet his gaze, let alone see what was in it.

Still, he'd mentioned that he'd found my strength interesting and that compliment went straight to my head like good champagne. And now that he has me in his grip, I'm clinging to it like an oyster with a piece of grit and polishing it into a pearl.

He's so strong, so powerful, and if he thinks I have strength and that he wants to test it, then what I want is to be tested. And to beat him.

His gaze is overwhelming in its power and I want to look away, but I can't. The force of his gravity is drawing me helplessly in, and I can hear someone breathing harshly and fast, and it's me. I know it's me.

"It hurts, doesn't it?" he asks.

I want to nod but I can't, not with the way he's holding my head. "Y-yes," I manage to force out, knowing better than to lie this time.

"Do you want me to stop?" There is no inflection in the words. It's as if he's asking me if I'd like a cup of tea.

I can't look anywhere but up at his face and so I try to read it, read him. Is this a challenge? A dare? Does he want me to say yes? Does he want me to fight?

"Don't think," he murmurs, his voice low and dark. "And don't try to second-guess me. What I want and my will are all that matters."

I heave in a breath, trying to get my head around the question, because if his will is all that matters, then why is he asking me what I want? "But....I....d-don't..." I try to get the words out, but my voice is shaking so much. "I don't... understand..."

"No, of course you don't." He leans down further so we're nose to nose and there is no escaping him. No escaping the delicious scent of his aftershave or the forceful hand in my hair, of the heat of his body so close to mine. "So, for future reference, the correct reply to that question is, *whatever you will, Master.*"

I open my mouth parrot the answer, but instead, he closes the distance between us and brushes his mouth over mine in the softest, most featherlight of kisses. Shock ripples through me. That's the last thing I was expecting and the contrast of his hot mouth with the punishing grip in my hair makes everything in me go tight. I want to lean into his kiss and I'm unable to stop myself as I do, but his fingers tighten as he lifts his mouth from mine, holding me in place.

"Keep still," he says. "You'll accept what you're given and nothing more."

I'm shivering, oddly bereft, as if he's taken a promised treat away from me and for no reason. My lips feel sensitized, the heat from his lingering, and all I want is for him to kiss me again and deeper, harder. But as he's shown me from the beginning, what I want doesn't matter, only what he does, and so I have to try and hide the longing in my gaze.

I know he sees it though, because that cruel mouth of his curves slightly, as if my desire amuses him. Then he lets me go, so suddenly that I nearly fall over. Rising to his full height, he turns and without a word he vanishes through the doorway, leaving me alone in the room.

It's as if a storm front has passed, all the electricity in the room draining away. My scalp is still tingling from the force of his grip and my lips burn. Every muscle in my body is tense, my skin drawn tight over my bones, and the throb between my thighs won't go away. I so desperately want him to touch me I can't think.

I look down at my hands, my fingers digging into my thighs as if I'm trying to hold onto something to stop from falling, and all I can think is that this is way more intense than I'd expected. *He* is way more intense than I'd expected, and I can't deny that it's testing me.

I could say my safe word if I wanted to, I know that, and I have to admit that I'm kind of tempted. I don't know if I want his particular brand of intense, or maybe it's more that I don't know if I'm ready for it.

You aren't and he told you that.

He did, but I didn't listen. Perhaps I should have.

It would be easy to slip out now. To grab my dress, shoes, and purse, and scuttle away like a frightened rabbit. Go back to my dreary apartment and sit there in the middle of the wreckage of all the dreams I had for myself, of getting my degree and getting started on a career in financial analysis, with a view to starting my own company. All of them gone because some fucking man decided he could help himself to my courage and strength and sense of self, leaving me panic-stricken and a mess.

A thread of fury winds through me at the thought, thick and hot, and something in me hardens. No, fuck leaving. I'm not running away just because this is intense. Maybe Mr. Fairfax is being deliberately mean because he wants me to run, but fuck him too. He also said I had strength, that he wants to test it, and if this is part of his test then I'm going to fucking ace it if it's the last fucking thing I do. I wasn't the class valedictorian in high school for nothing.

So I sit there, my fingers still digging into my thighs, unmoving. Determined not to move even an inch so when he gets back he'll have nothing to complain about. But time begins to move weirdly. I feel as if I've been sitting here for an hour, but maybe it isn't an hour. Maybe it's only been ten minutes. Or five.

I stare at the doorway but it remains stubbornly empty, and I have to breathe through a strange and burgeoning panic. Perhaps he's gone. Perhaps he went out and left me here and he won't come back till much later. Or perhaps he won't come back at all.

There is no sound anywhere, the apartment perfectly insulated. I can see the lights of the city through the plate glass windows and other buildings surrounding us. Can they see me? Can they see me sitting here naked and trembling?

Time gets even weirder, slowing and elongating like hot taffy, and I can hear my own breath rushing in and out of my lungs. And somehow everything feels as if it's getting tenser and tenser, and I'm going to scream if I'm not careful.

But just before I do, suddenly he comes back into the room carrying a wooden box, and all the tension in the room ratchets up even higher. He's bringing that electricity back with him, too, and I can feel sparking all over my skin.

I sit up straighter, expecting him to glance in my direction, but he doesn't, and that makes the ember of stubborn anger sitting in my gut burn hotter. Fine, if that's how he wants to play it then, I'll show him. I'm ready. I was born fucking ready.

Mr. Fairfax sets the box down on the floor next to the low slab of granite that is the coffee table, then begins taking things out. I watch him, my mouth getting drier and drier as I suddenly realize what all those things are — I've seen them in the web searches I did.

A black leather flogger. A red ball gag. A pair of jeweled clamps with a fine chain linking them. A heavy duty looking blindfold. Some black cuffs. A vibrator.

Hard Discipline

He says nothing once they're all displayed, merely straightening and then going over to a sleek drinks cabinet of dark wood, taking out a tumbler and a bottle. He opens the bottle, pours a measure of golden liquid into the tumbler, then strolls back to the coffee table and looks meditatively down at the toys he's laid out.

My breathing sounds shaky in the endless silence and I find I can't look away from the toys or from him. Is he thinking about which one he's going to use on me? Because obviously they're for me, aren't they? A shiver moves through me, a strange mixture of fear, desire, dread, and a breathless anticipation. My brain won't stop picturing him using all those toys on me in all kinds of ways, and I don't know whether I'm terrified or turned on.

He doesn't move, sipping slowly from his tumbler, and time seems to stretch out the way it did before—becoming elastic and syrupy. My brain is moving faster and I'm starting to pant, because I don't want him to use those things on me. *I don't.* I was hurt in the attack, my hands scraped against the brick wall of the building as that bastard held me against it, forcing me into immobility. I hadn't thought all the bondage stuff would be a problem, but now it's staring me in the face, I realize it very much is a problem. And I don't want it to be.

I don't want to be afraid, but I am.

"I can hear you breathing, sub," Mr. Fairfax says, still looking down at the coffee table. "You sound afraid. See something you don't like?"

Is it a rhetorical question? Do I answer?

"You may answer," he continues, his attention on the toys even as he reads my mind.

"Y-yes," I stutter hoarsely.

"You want to give me your safe word?"

"No." This time there is no stutter.

Finally he turns and glances at me, his gaze a fierce blue flame and sucks all the air from my lungs. I can't read the expression on his face, but...is that approval? Is he pleased?

He takes another sip of his drink, still studying me. "Pick one," he says. "Pick a toy you'd like me to use."

I blink, unsure, because he's really going to let me decide on a toy? That seems very generous of him. But his expression remains enigmatic and it seems as if he's waiting for me to choose, so I look at the array of toys, my breath shuddering in and out. They all look little frightening if not outright painful, so I go for the one I'm at least familiar with.

"The v-vibrator," I say, my voice husky in the silence of the room.

His gaze is still pinned to mine as he nods slowly. "A fine choice," he murmurs. Then he knocks back his drink, puts the tumbler down on the coffee table, and picks up the jeweled clamps instead. "But again, the correct answer to any question I put to you is, *whatever you will, Master.*"

Fuck. That was another test?

And you failed it.

I lick my dry lips, my eyes prickling for some reason. "I-I'm sorry. I should—"

"You'll learn," he interrupts, holding the jeweled clamps in his hands as he comes over to where I'm kneeling. He crouches down in front of me, searching my face with the kind of focused intensity he seems to bring to everything he does. "You can cry, sub," he says. "It's hard when you disappoint people isn't it?"

I blink furiously, because I don't want to cry. I've gotten used to failing people over the last couple of years, so why the fuck it matters to me so much that I failed his stupid test is anyone's guess. And who cares if I cry in front of him anyway? I already have, so it's not like he hasn't seen my tears.

"You're used to succeeding," he goes on, still staring intently at me. "Luc told me. In fact you're a regular little high achiever aren't you?" He holds the clamps delicately. "In which case here's another test for you."

And before I can do anything, he fastens the clamps to my throbbing nipples.

10

Gideon

She gasps aloud as I fasten each jeweled clamp gently on her pale, pretty nipples. They're already hard so this will hurt, but I wanted to see what her tits would look like with them on. And indeed, they look as fucking beautiful as I thought they would.

The pressure is slight, enough for a beginner, and from the shaken hissing of her breath as I adjust the tension, it's more than enough for her now. Her eyes have gone huge, her body trembling as I shift back to look at my handiwork.

I've been hard on her, it's true, but that's the kind of Master I am. I mess with a sub's head and set her off balance so that the only steady ground for her is me.

The kiss I gave her was just one example. She wasn't expecting it, especially given how hard I was holding her hair — giving the rough with the smooth can really unsettle a sub so deliciously. I don't normally kiss subs, though,

Hard Discipline

because that involves a level of intimacy or closeness that I don't enjoy. However, my instinct told me it would put her off balance, so I went with it, and indeed it did. What was a little disturbing was the strange urge I had to keep kissing her, which I never, ever experience. Her lips were soft and lush, and I just knew that if I parted them with my tongue, her mouth would be hot and sweet.

But I told her the truth when I said I was into denial. Subs think that means denying them what they want, and it is, but I also deny myself. It builds the tension, builds the electricity, builds the hunger to a screaming point, which then makes the orgasm even more intense. Both for her and for me.

I took my time choosing which toys I was going to use for that reason too. I wanted to mess with her head even more by getting her to sit in the living area on her own. Time can play tricks on you in those kinds of situations and I could tell the moment I walked back into the room that it had played those tricks on her.

I checked on her out of the corner of my eye as I walked over to the coffee table with the box, and it was enough to see the flood of relief in her face as she watched me. I already knew what she was thinking, her busy mind going over and over where I'd gone and for how long, and perhaps I'd abandoned her. That's good, though. I want her to keep thinking about me, because eventually she'll learn that she doesn't have to think. That all she has to do is give me her complete and utter trust and in return I'll give her pleasure beyond her wildest dreams.

I still need to get into her head more though, find out her weak points and vulnerabilities. She's sensitive about failure, I could see it in her eyes when she picked out the vibrator and I told her that wasn't the right answer. Makes sense considering what Lucas told me about her acing most of her classes at Yale before she dropped out. She's an anxious high achiever who wants to please, but is also as stubborn as fuck.

I could see just how stubborn when I came back into the room and she was kneeling there, radiating determination. She'd had a battle with herself, no doubt, about whether to leave or to stay, and in the end her stubbornness won out.

You were hoping she'd go.

I push the thought away as I rise to my feet again and go back to the coffee table for the other clamp. Why would I hope that she'd leave? Yes, she's young and my son's ex, and a submissive new to the scene. I've warned her what I'm like and she accepted that, and I have to admit I'm enjoying this more than I thought I would. But that's all.

She's different though, you can't deny it.

I certainly fucking do deny it. I've never wanted to train a sub before and sure, there's something… possessive in me that likes the idea of training her to suit my needs alone, but that's a timing thing. Gabrielle's birthday and all that shit. And yes, she did push, and that alone would be enough for me to refuse, but I didn't, so that part's on me. It's not for any other reason.

I pick up the third clamp and go back to where she's kneeling. The fine chain linking the jeweled clamps on her nipples hangs between her breasts, glittering like the jewels as they rise and fall with her heightened breathing.

A flush has risen into her cheeks, making the silver of her eyes look even darker as they cling to mine. The pulse at the base of her throat is racing and down between her thighs, that little pussy of hers is slick and glistening.

She's a fucking delicious sight, I have to say.

I crouch once again in front of her, but I say nothing as I

attach the third clamp to the O-ring that links the two currently on her nipples. Then I look down between her thighs at all that wet, pink flesh. "This one is going to hurt," I tell her as I look back into her eyes. "But I think you can deal, can't you, sub? You can answer."

"Y-y-yes," she manages. "M-Master."

"Very prettily said," I murmur, noting how her flush deepens at the compliment, and getting a kick of satisfaction out of her response myself. I am sparing with my compliments and praise, because it makes it much more intense for the sub when they finally earn one from me. Obviously being praised is something she likes, so I file that away for future reference.

I look down between her thighs. "Spread your pussy for me. Let me see that hard little clit."

She hesitates only a second before dropping her shaking hands between her thighs, holding apart the soft, pink folds. I can smell her, the sweetness of roses and the musky scent of feminine arousal, and it's fucking hot. Much hotter than it should be, quite frankly, but my dick disagrees. It likes the smell of her, wants all that tight, slick flesh around it, and it's insistent. In fact, I can't think of when my cock was last so fucking demanding.

I ignore it, though, because no matter how insistent it is, it's not getting what it wants, not yet. Instead, I gently close the third clamp around the base of her clit. She gives a soft little cry, her body jerking and shivering as I adjust the pressure, keeping tabs on her expression all the while.

I want her on the border of pleasure and pain, and to test that border. I want to see what kind of strength she has and how I can use that to drive her out of her mind and give that busy brain of hers a rest, because I can see it spinning and spinning in her eyes.

This is what she needs, even if she doesn't know that herself yet. She's looking for someone to stop her thinking, to let her exist in the moment where the past and the future don't exist. Where there is no success or failure, only pleasure.

"Does it hurt, sub?" I ask.

"Y-yes." Her eyes have filled with helpless tears and I know she's fighting to keep them at bay, I can see the battle going on inside her.

"Too much?"

She swallows. "I c-can handle it."

I stare into her liquid gray eyes to see if she's giving me the truth, and she is. She doesn't want to disappoint me or fail me, I can see that also, but she'll learn that it's not her success or failure that matters right here and now. It's mine. Because I'm the one in charge.

"You can cry," I tell her, giving her permission to weep and scream and let out whatever emotion is inside her. "You know I like your tears."

She swallows yet again and shakes, the tears beginning to fall, and I can tell she doesn't like it. That even though I gave her permission to cry, she hasn't given herself permission, yet they fall anyway.

"Eyes on me," I order as she tries to look away. "Always on me."

She's trembling harder as she meets my gaze and I hold hers pinned to mine. Then I reach out and take the chains that link the clamps and I tug on them, adding to the sensations she's feeling. A cry escapes her and her back arches, and I look into her darkening eyes, seeing the pleasure/pain burning bright there. She likes this, even though it hurts as much as it pleases. I tug a little harder, because she's a fighter, this one, and fucking delicious draped in my jewels and chains with the most sensitive parts of her body under my direct control.

"You can say your safe word," I remind her. "You can say it any time."

She's thinking about it, I know she is, but the moment I say the words, I can see the determination inside her harden, the strength I've already seen in her, rising to the surface. Her jaw tightens, her lips compressing, flames glittering in her eyes.

Fuck, this woman is not just an anxious overthinker or a victim. There's more to her than that, and for the first time, it's not only the Master who wants to know more about her but the man, too. I want to know happened to her during the attack that made her drop out of college. That turned her into a pale, colorless version of the woman kneeling in front of me now, all pink and silver, white and red, with eyes like fucking molten mercury.

Because *this* is her, I know that already. The real her. Panting and shivering, yet strong and determined, so fucking determined....

"N-no," she stammers, but there is iron in the word.

Brave sub.

I check her over, to make sure she's physically okay, then I nod. "More it is, then." And I tug on the chains, pulling at them with a controlled force, enough to cause her a little more pain and a little more pleasure but not hard enough to cancel the pleasure out entirely.

Another shaken cry escapes her, the tears sliding down her cheeks. She lifts a hand to wipe them away, but I grab her wrist, stopping her. "No," I order. "I want your fucking tears, sub. I want your screams and your cries. I want your strength and your determination. I want everything, understand?"

She takes a sobbing breath and nods jerkily, but I don't let go of her wrist. Instead I bring her palm to my mouth and press a kiss in the center of it, watching her as I do and tugging again on the chains with my other hand. She rewards me with another cry, her eyes glazed, her cheeks wet.

Her skin tastes salty and sweet and delicious, and again desire kicks hard inside me, unexpectedly powerful. A part of me wants to give her a climax, because she's so fucking hot and so fucking strong. This is all new to her, the clamps, the obedience, the pain mixed with pleasure, and she's taken it and dealt with it all with courage.

A lesser woman, knowing what was in store for her, might have disappeared the moment I left the room, but Odette didn't. Her curiosity and strength were stronger than her fear and they won that battle. I have nothing but respect for that.

She was wasted on Lucas.

The thought comes without prompting and I find myself agreeing, because yes she fucking was. He didn't see what I see right now, burning in front of me. An iron strength. The passion of a woman who'll go out and get whatever she wants, and fuck anyone who gets in her way.

Gabrielle wasn't like that. She was gentler, kinder. Gave me a fuck-load more grace than I deserved, not that I'm the same young punk that I was back then. As I've gotten older, I've gotten harder, more selfish, less tolerant of bullshit. If Gabrielle met me now, she'd probably think I was the world's biggest asshole.

This woman, though. I'm intrigued, I can't lie. With all of this spirit, why did she drop out? Why did she let some asshole strip all of that away from her? And what is she looking for so desperately that she thinks she can get it from me?

"Do you want to come, sub?" I demand, tugging again on the chains

She gives a hiccupping sob. "W-whatever you w-will, M-master."

Satisfaction surges inside me, a lick of heat that lights a fire in my veins that I always get when a sub bends herself to my will. But this is more intense somehow, and I realize it's because she's not a practiced sub who knows what to say in order to get what she wants, or a familiar play partner spouting a rote response. And I've forgotten what it's like to see a sub say the words, and mean them. To know that she wants to please not only the Dom, but me. It's a gesture of trust, whether she knows it or not, and it's honest. She's listened to me, taken my lesson on board, and while she's still afraid, she's saying it anyway, because she means it.

That in itself deserves a reward. So letting go of her wrist, I slide my hand behind the back of her head and pull her forward, until those soft red lips meet mine.

And I give her more of the kiss that we've both been wanting.

11

Odette

I'm in agony, but I don't know whether it's an agony of pain or an agony of pleasure. Both have become one, so intertwined I can't separate one from the other. The pressure of the clamps on my sensitive nipples is bad enough, but the one he settled around my clit is almost overwhelming.

He told me it would hurt and it does, yet I feel as if I could also come at any moment and I can't get my head around that. It's weird how pleasure and pain can be so locked together, because I always assumed pleasure was pleasure, and pain was only pain. Yet when he attached those clamps and pulled on the chains, the pain and pleasure fused, becoming something so intense that part of me wants to scream my safe word, while the rest of me wants to scream *more*.

His blue gaze was everything, the whole world, and

when he told me he wanted my tears I couldn't stop them from falling. It was kind of liberating in a way, because it was clear my tears didn't bother him. They bothered Lucas, though. He never said anything explicitly, but I know he didn't like hearing about the attack or about my feelings around it, because it made him angry. He didn't understand that I didn't need him to do anything, I only wanted him to listen.

My parents, too, had no patience for my fears and so I learned to keep them bottled up and to distract myself with school, sublimate my anxieties into getting good grades, and pushing harder to get better. I never took failure well and neither did my parents, so Mr. Fairfax sitting there watching me weep without judgement just felt...freeing.

Then he grabbed my wrist when I tried to wipe my tears away and the kiss he pressed into my palm felt like he'd lit a fire inside me. The warmth of his mouth on my sensitized flesh added to the agony of sensation, and then that look in his hard blue eyes, as if he could see something in me that I hadn't known was there...

God. I was ready to do anything he wanted. Anything at all. And I remembered what he told me so when he asked me if I wanted to come, there was only one response I could give him. Yes, I fucking wanted to come. I burned for it. But only if he wanted me to.

I wasn't expecting him to kiss me again, so I'm in shock as he pulls me in and his mouth covers mine. But it's not the same kiss as before. That was light, gentle, and this is... not either of those things. His tongue pushes into my mouth, taking what he wants the way a conqueror takes a castle, without mercy and without quarter. His fingers wind into my hair, holding me in place as he ravages me. I sense that he doesn't want me to respond, he only wants to master me, and that's good because even if I wanted to, I can't kiss him back, not with him exploring my mouth as if he owns it. He tugs on those fucking chains at the same time, too, the heat of the kiss and the agonizing pull of the clamps making me burn like I have a fever.

I give a sobbing moan against his mouth and then his teeth are sinking into my bottom lip, giving me a sharp nip that turns my moan into a wail. I can't bear this and yet I want more. I want more of his kiss, more pressure on the clamps, more pain, more everything, because this is the most intensely alive I've ever felt. And despite being under his command, I'm also so inexplicably free.

I have pleased him — I saw the glitter of heat in his eyes when I said *your will, Master* — and the way he's kissing me...

I think he likes this as much as I do and a burst of confidence fills me. A confidence I lost two years ago, that shattered and broke that night outside the bar. It's not the same pure confidence that I would conquer the world like I did when I graduated high school, but it's there. A fragile hope of something better. So, I lean into the kiss, not demanding or insisting, but taking what he gives me, letting him know that I am here for his will and his alone.

He tastes of the alcohol he was drinking earlier— a good scotch, rich and strong— and something else, a flavor intrinsic to him and it makes me hungry. Everything about him makes me hungry.

He tugs at the chains again, sending lightning strikes of pleasure/pain radiating out from my nipples and my clit, and I cry out again against his lips. Abruptly, he pulls away, one hand still buried in my hair, and in a series of deft, practiced movements, he takes the clamps off my distended nipples and clit. As soon as the pressure disappears, the blood rushes back in and it hurts like a bastard. Tears roll down my cheeks and I whimper like a wounded animal, but his mouth is back and he's kissing me again, slower this time, deeper, as if he's tasting me, relishing me.

Then I feel his hand reach down between my thighs, to where I'm so sensitive, and he's sliding one finger into me. The sensation is so intense I give a muffled scream against his lips, but he doesn't stop, sliding another finger in and then a third. I'm so wet there's no resistance, and when he starts to work them in and out of me, the pleasure is like a blade slicing through me. He doesn't touch my swollen clit, but he doesn't need to, the friction and the feeling of being stretched by his fingers is everything. I can feel an orgasm barreling down on me like a freight train and I don't think I can stop it.

"No," he warns against my lips. "Don't you fucking come.

Automatically I fight the urge, panting and sobbing, but he doesn't stop the movement of his fingers and it's relentless, and no matter how hard I struggle against it there's no stopping the climax.

It's like a tsunami, gathering strength and power as it builds, and then it's rolling over me, the force of the pleasure shattering me as if I'm made of crystal.

I scream and scream against his mouth, shaking and shaking, the broken pieces of me rubbing against one another and magnifying the intensity. I lose track of where I am, of who I am, completely at the mercy of the ecstasy shaking me apart.

His hands withdraw, but his arms are closing around me and lifting me, and I'm only half-aware of being carried over to the couch. I expect him to set me down on it, but he doesn't. Instead, he sits with me in his lap and wraps a blanket around me, then he holds me as I shake and tremble with the aftershocks, tears still rolling down my face for no reason that I can see. He's so hot, his chest hard, his arms strong, and I'm enclosed in them like a secret he wants to keep.

My head rests against the warm stone of his chest, and I can hear his heart beating, slow and steady. I let the sound of it fill my head, and soon my sobs fade and my breathing becomes more even, matching the beat of his heart.

For a few blissful moments, I think of nothing at all, floating in a wonderful post-orgasmic haze that I never want to end.

Then he says, "Wait here. I'll be back."

He eases me onto the sofa cushions and vanishes through the doorway again, but he doesn't leave me for long this time. I've barely registered he left before he's back, and once again I'm in his lap, held in his arms.

"Drink this," he instructs and holds a glass of water to my lips.

I don't even think about disobeying, sipping at it, letting the cool water ease my throat, a little painful after all that screaming. This must be the aftercare I've read about, when a Dom provides physical comfort and reassurance after a scene. Well, if so, I like it very much.

He makes me drink the whole glass and while I'm sipping, I become conscious of something very hard beneath my butt. My God, if that's his cock — and really, what else could it be? — then he's huge. Also, he must be desperate for release, and yet he's making no move on me. It's as if it doesn't matter to him and part of me is turned on by his control, while another part is exceptionally pleased with myself that I've got him in this state at all.

After I've drained the glass, I rest my head against his shoulder and look up at him. For once he's not looking at me, staring off into the distance instead, and slowly I become aware of how tense he is. His expression is about as readable as a lump of granite, and I'm suddenly desperate to know what he's thinking. Does he not like this part? This aftercare thing? He doesn't give the impression of a man who is used to giving comfort, I guess, considering how hard he is, yet he's doing it for me anyway. Perhaps he feels he has to?

"I'm sorry," I say, my voice husky in the silence. "I'll be okay in a moment."

Instantly, he glances down at me. "Why are you apologizing?"

"Because I came when you told me not to. And also...you don't have to hold me like this if you don't want to."

He's staring at me, not in the way he stares when he's giving instructions, but as if what I just said has surprised him. "Why do you think I don't like holding you?"

"You're tense. In fact your whole body is tight." I shift, ready to move away, but his arms tighten around me, and this time it's my turn to be surprised. "What?"

"Did I tell you to move, sub?" he says roughly.

"But you don't like—"

"Whose will is important here?"

I take a little breath. "Yours."

"That's right. And if I want to hold you, I fucking will, understand?"

I stare up at his hard features, the force of his command beating me down, making me want to curl up against him and not push. But I can't stop myself. "Then why are you so tense?"

A muscle flicks in his hard jaw. "I don't have to explain myself to you."

He's so intimidating and I don't know why I'm pushing

him or what I answer I want him to give. All I know is that he's tense and I want to help. "If you need something from this sub, Master, you can have it," I say hesitantly. "You can have anything."

That muscle flicks again and I can see something glitter in his blue stare. Something hot and bright and sharp. It gives me a whole body shiver, and I'm abruptly aware once again of my nakedness, and how the blanket feels against my skin. How the tips of my breasts and my clit are aching and tender, and yet the anticipation and delicious fear is building once again—my body desperate for more.

He wants you.

A flush of heat goes through me as I realize it. The truth is laid bare in his gaze and satisfaction kicks hard in my gut in response. I can't hide it, so he sees— and abruptly he rips the blanket away from me, turning me in his lap so I'm facing away, my back to his front. He snakes an arm around my neck, strong fingers gripping me just below my chin, his palm pressing against the pulse in my throat. It's not a chokehold, but his grip is like iron all the same. I'm caught and held there, shaking once again, my breathing out of control.

"Fucking sub," he growls in my ear, his breath warm against my skin. "Of course I can have anything. I'm the Master here. I can have whatever I fucking want from you." His grip tightens. "Perhaps I'll fuck you right now, right here. Because I can have anything I want. Isn't that right, sub?"

I've pissed him off, I can hear it in the roughness of his voice and in the tension pulled tight in his body, and a small part of me is panicking, expecting violence. Because that's what men do when they're angry.

"I-I'm sorry, M-Master," I gasp, unable to hide the note of real fear in my voice. "I-I shouldn't have pushed—"

"I'm not going to hurt you," he interrupts, his voice hard and deep. "Don't panic, just breathe."

Instinctively I obey, and as I do I realize that his grip on my throat is firm but not too much. I can breathe with ease. He won't hurt me. Of course he won't. His control over himself and me is perfect.

"Tell me what happened," he says and it's definitely an order.

But my brain is still flailing and I don't understand. "W-what?"

"The attack," he clarifies. "What happened to you?"

I don't want to talk about it and I don't want to tell him, and he must know that because he continues, "I need to know, sub. You panicked just then and I didn't hear a safe word. That means you were too frightened to say it and I can't have that."

He's not wrong, I didn't even think about saying *red*. "Please don't send me away," I babble, because he's going to isn't he? He won't want to deal with my fear and anxiety, no one does, and I can't—

"I'm not going to send you away." His dark, deep voice cuts through my whirling thoughts, sharp as a scalpel. "But I will if you don't tell me."

All I can think is that I don't want him to do that, so I open my mouth and it all comes flooding out. "I went to a bar for a drink with some friends, and I drank too much. I wanted to go home early to recover because I had to study, so I left before them. It was dark and there was a guy waiting in an alley beside the bar, and he jumped me." I inhale shakily then go on, "I-I think he was angry and he kept calling me names. He punched me a couple of times, then pushed me against the brick wall and started tearing at my clothes." My eyes are filling with tears again, remembering my own sense of powerlessness at how weak I was against him, and how I knew that there was no way to stop him from doing anything he wanted. "I c-couldn't stop him, I was too weak. And so..." I swallow. "I didn't even try." It sounds so insignificant when I say it all aloud. Thousands of women have had this experience, I'm not unique in any way, and I'm angry with myself that I let it affect me so deeply. "It's so stupid," I say hoarsely. "I let it ruin my whole career and my life, and I—"

"Stop." Mr. Fairfax interrupts me again and his fingers move against my skin testing his hold on my throat, and for some reason, this time it reassures me rather than panics me. "You didn't *let* anything happen, understand? Some cowardly motherfucker saw an opportunity and took it, that's all." His lips are near my ear, brushing gently against my skin. "He didn't take your strength or your determination, it's still there, sub. Because if it wasn't, you wouldn't be naked in my lap, about to be fucked into insensibility."

That shouldn't be hot, it really shouldn't, and it shouldn't be reassuring either. Yet it's both. Mr. Fairfax who is older, richer, and far more experienced than I am, not to mention exponentially more powerful, thinks I'm strong and determined, and he wouldn't say that if he didn't believe it. It certainly feels like the truth. I mean, he's right, isn't he? I thought about leaving, yet I didn't. I stayed. I was determined to.

"B-But...." I stammer, still doubting.

"What I say goes," he says, one thumb stroking up and down on the side of my neck. "So if I say you're brave and strong then you are."

Hard Discipline

I close my eyes. It can't be that easy, can it? To just... believe him? I want to so badly.

"Trust me, sub," he murmurs, reading my mind yet again, his warm breath on my neck. "That's all you have to do."

And I haven't, I suddenly understand. A small, frightened piece of me has been holding back, too afraid to give him that last little bit of trust. But... maybe I don't have to be frightened anymore. Or maybe I can be, but I can also surrender everything to him anyway. Give him all of my trust and let him do what he wants with me. He won't hurt me, not like my attacker did, and while everything he's done has been challenging, that's a good thing. I've avoided being challenged for a long time, because I never felt equal to it. But I feel equal to it with him, because he believes I am.

So I relax, surrendering everything I am to him. "Yes, Master," I breathe.

His body is a furnace at my back, hard and hot, his grip on my throat firm. "Good girl," he says, and I can hear in his voice that somehow he knows what I've just given him, and that it pleases him. "That wasn't so hard, was it?" Without warning, he slips a hand between my spread thighs, his fingers exploring the slick folds of my pussy. I'm already wet and my clit is still so achingly sensitive from the clamps that when he strokes it, then pinches it, a hoarse scream rips from my throat.

"I'm going to fuck you," he murmurs roughly against my neck. "But since you've already had an orgasm, you're not allowed another. So if you come, I'll punish you."

Dimly, I'm astonished that I'm even capable of pleasure after that last orgasm and the conversation we've just had. Yet with only a few words and rough touches, he's got me building to another climax already. But I'm not going to be able to obey him, because if he's going to fuck me the way he said he would, I'm done.

Except I have no chance to think further, because while one hand grips my throat, I can hear him undoing his zipper with the other. Then comes another rustle of fabric and the hot, hard head of his cock is pressing my wet flesh. I gasp as he pushes into me, because he's not gentle, and he's huge, and I'm stretched wide. His grip on my throat tightens, keeping my back firmly against his chest, his other hand spreading me as he pushes in deeper. I shudder and let out another scream of agonized pleasure, because it's so good. So fucking good. I don't even think I need him to move. I'm going to come the moment he's fully inside me.

"You fucking did this," he growls against my neck and I can feel the edge of his teeth against my skin. "You got me hot, sub, and so you'll deal with the fucking consequences. You'll take all of me and I don't care if it hurts. All I care about is that you don't. Fucking. Come."

Then his hand around my throat grips me hard, while the other slides beneath my left thigh, pulling my leg wider. He thrusts inside me even deeper and I sink my teeth into my bottom lip, trying to hold back the shattering pleasure.

I'm shaking now and he's moving, his cock huge inside me, and I'm crying again because I want to obey him but I can't and we both know it. The pressure and the friction is tearing me apart. He lets go of my leg, his fingers sliding over my agonizingly sensitive clit, and he pinches— making me wail as the orgasm smashes through every shred of resistance I have left, crushing me beneath its weight.

He doesn't stop though. He keeps thrusting, keeps fingering my clit. "Why is it so hard to obey a simple instruction?" he asks roughly. "Try again, sub." He nips the side of my neck at the same time as he gives my clit another pinch, and just like that the aftershocks of the climax I just had, build relentlessly to another.

"I—I c-can't," I babble hoarsely.

"Like I said." His hips thrust up, his cock sliding deeper before pulling back. "I don't care." Another thrust, the slide of his dick pushing me implacably higher and higher.

I'm moaning helplessly now, trying again to hold back the orgasm, but I can't, not with the way he's playing with my clit and constant drive of his cock. Holding back this orgasm is just as impossible as trying to hold back the last. I feel as if I'm trying to hold back a hurricane with only my bare hands.

I put my head back, opening my mouth to scream, but he's tilting my head back and covering my lips with his, taking the scream from my throat as the orgasm smashes me apart and drowns me, leaving me with nothing to hold onto except for him.

12

Gideon

I've got my hand around her throat, her pulse beating frantically against my palm, her pussy clenching around my cock as she screams into my mouth. She's coming again, as I made sure she would— never mind my orders— shaking and shaking against me, which only adds to burn of hunger in my blood.

Subs give me their trust all the time, so her surrendering to me the way she just did shouldn't make me even hotter for her. But it did and I am. I felt her fear the moment I put my hand around her throat and she tensed up. And I knew it wasn't the delicious fear of a sub anticipating what she'd get from Dom, but something far colder and more real.

I'd been annoyed that she'd noticed my tension during the aftercare, but in that moment I'd shoved aside my temper, because her fear was a serious issue and it needed to be addressed. I knew it could only be about the attack and that I had to get the truth from her before we went any further, so I commanded her to tell me. Which she did, without hesitation.

Hearing about it did not help my temper, but as with anything that happens during a scene, I pushed my own emotions aside. She needed reassurance from me, that was clear, as was the fact that she still didn't trust me, not fully.

I'm the Dom, I'm in charge, so when a sub needs reassurance, that's what I give. But she needed more than empty words — I could hear the notes of anger and self-loathing in her voice — so I told her what was true. That her strength and courage were still there, that he hadn't taken them away from her. That she'd always had them otherwise she wouldn't be here. As soon as I'd told her that, I realized that not only did the Master mean it, the man did too. I should have pulled away then, put some distance between us because the man and the Master are two different people to me, except I didn't. I couldn't. It would hurt her and she didn't need to be hurt any more than she already had been.

Instead, I leaned into it, getting that last shred of trust from her, and when she finally surrendered to me— surrendered completely— I felt the pleasure and triumph of it in my chest, in my head, in my blood, in my cock. Every-fucking-where. And I was desperate in a way I've never been before. So desperate to be inside her, I couldn't wait.

And I can always wait. Always. Desire has never gotten the better of me before so why a sub finally giving me the ultimate gift of her trust got the better of me tonight, I have no fucking idea.

Perhaps it was giving her that orgasm with the clamps, after she was so goddamn brave with it. Or maybe it was that kiss I gave her as she came, tasting so fucking delicious, her mouth hot and sweet and her scream of release when she came an added bite. Perhaps it was picking up her shuddering body and taking her to the couch, wrapping her in a blanket, and holding her until she quietened. It couldn't have been the aftercare, because I dislike it intensely. That's not because of the subs, it's because of how it reminds me of caring for Gabrielle in those last few weeks and the emotional agony of not being able to make her better.

You know why you couldn't wait.

I shove that thought away, back into the darkness it came from, concentrating instead on the feel of her pussy hot and wet around my cock. I haven't fucked a sub in a while, that's probably why she's brought me to a knife-edge, nothing more.

Her mouth is hot beneath mine and she tastes of apples, tart and sweet.

I'm going to have to punish her for coming twice in a row against my express permission, and knowing that adds more spice to the heat already climbing inside me. She's still convulsing in my grip, but I don't let up, thrusting deep and hard inside her tight little cunt until my own orgasm explodes in my head like fucking firework. It makes me growl into her mouth, nipping and biting at her bottom lip as I come.

It takes me far longer than it should to recover, and for at least a couple of minutes all I'm aware of is the tremble of her body against mine and her frantic breathing. Then my Master's instinct kicks in and I pull out of her, turning her so I can check she's okay, that I haven't hurt her.

Her cheeks are flushed and wet with tears, her mascara has run, and she looks utterly ravaged. She's beautiful, especially with the red marks of my fingers on the pale skin of her throat. She's breathing easily, though. I run my hand gently over her, conducting a visual check on her nipples and clit to make sure she's not still hurting, but apart from another convulsive shiver, everything looks good and she doesn't seem to be in any pain.

She's gone lax against me, her lashes fluttering closed. She looks young and vulnerable, and the fact that she's lying against me so trustingly makes something in my chest tighten. She's new and untried, and perhaps I should have been more mindful of her.

You didn't use a fucking condom either.

Ah, Christ. I didn't.

I wrap her in the blanket again and settle her on the couch, then leave the room, heading for the bathroom on this level. The lights flick on automatically as I enter and go over to the vanity. I run some water into the basin and splash it on my face, trying to clear my fucking head, then I grip the sides of the basin and stare at my reflection in the mirror.

I didn't use a condom and I *always* use a condom. It's not that pregnancy or an STD is an issue — everyone who uses The Club app has regular doctor's checkups and birth control is mandatory. It's mainly so that anyone who wants to go bareback can without fuss, but that's not a kink of mine. There's an element of control and distance with a condom, and I prefer that. I've never, ever *forgotten* one. Until now.

The man in the mirror stares back, his jaw tight, his gaze hard. This sub is getting under his skin and he doesn't like it.

Send her home.

I should. But then that would admit that she's getting to me and that's a loss of control I can't tolerate. A sub always has the ultimate control, because the whole point of a scene is their pleasure, and I've never had an issue with that. It's how it should be. But this is different. This feel as if she's stolen some power from me, some power I didn't intend to give her, and now I'm not sure I can get it back.

She only has power if you let her take it.

True. In which case I need to get a fucking grip and make sure the Master is fully in command. I do not second-guess myself and I'm not about to start now.

Pushing myself away from the basin, I gather a few soft cloths and run them under the warm water before squeezing them out. Then I go back into the living area and over to the couch.

Odette is curled up beneath the blanket, her eyes closed. She's breathing deeply and evenly, but I know she's not asleep, only recovering. I'm not a gentle man, yet I attempt to be gentle as I unwrap her. She makes a sleepy-sounding protest but doesn't resist as I spread her legs and run the warm cloth between them. A breath goes out of her, her slight, pale body still lax as I clean her up. She watches me but says nothing and I can tell from her dilated pupils that she's probably had her first encounter with subspace and is still flying.

I don't look into her eyes this time, directing my attention to her body, doing another visual check. She's far too thin and I wonder if she's been eating properly, and yet—

You're starting to think like you did when Gabrielle was sick.

A cold wave of realization passes over me. This is why I don't do aftercare, because of that same fucking reason, and I know this. I did everything I could for her, even the difficult physical things that left her with precious little pride or dignity. I made sure I gave both of those back to her in her last weeks, and I'm doing something similar now.

Except Odette isn't sick, nor is she my wife.

"What is it?"

Her voice is soft and husky and it jolts me into meeting her gaze. Deep in the tarnished silver of her eyes I see something soft and concerned, and there's a slight crease in her smooth forehead, her pale brows drawn together.

The cold seeps through me. She must have seen my expression— no one has been able read me, not since Gabrielle —and I don't like that she has.

"Did I ask you to speak sub?" I ask flatly, putting her back in her place.

She flushes and her lashes lower in submission. "No, Master."

It should please me that she obeyed me and with my proper title, but I don't feel pleased. I feel as if I've done something wrong, though I know I haven't.

I've given this woman more orgasms in the space of an hour than I've ever given any sub over the course of entire evening, so why I feel chastened I have no fucking idea. What I do know is that I'm turning her into more of a big deal than she needs to be.

I continue to run the cloth over her, and she sighs, giving a sensual little stretch. It's entirely unselfconscious, and I find myself wanting to keep stroking her soft skin, keep touching her until I make her sigh just like that again and again. But she needs a break and something to eat, so I open my mouth to tell her what I'm going to do, except that's not what comes out. "I don't do much aftercare," I hear myself say instead, still stroking her. "Because I cared for my wife when she was sick and I don't like the reminder."

Odette doesn't move or speak, but her lashes flutter, the only sign of her reaction.

There is a moment of silence and unexpectedly I feel the weight of it this time, because it's not a silence I initiated with the purpose of reading a sub. Oddly, it's as if she's giving what I told her some time, acknowledging the weight of the subject.

Then, just when I'm on the verge of taking command again, because I don't fucking like what I'm feeling right now, her lashes lift and she reaches up, brushing my cheekbone with the tips of her fingers. She doesn't speak but I see what's in her eyes. Sympathy. Concern. And strangely, understanding.

Her touch is gentle, yet electric. It's been a long time since a sub has touched me, a long time since *anyone* has touched me. Sometimes I'll fuck a sub or let her suck me off, but I use that as a reward for good behavior. It's not something I generally allow and I certainly never seek out a sub's touch for comfort's sake, yet I sense that comfort is exactly what Odette is giving me now. I should punish her for touching me without asking, but strangely, I don't have the appetite for it.

Instead, I close my fingers around her wrist and hold it gently, and I don't pull it away. It's my gaze that subs can't meet. I never have a problem with theirs, and yet I'm having a problem holding hers now. I can't bear the understanding her eyes, yet a part of me is hungry for it, a need that burns in my chest.

But this little sub, this inexperienced young woman, this pale waif of a girl, looks away first, allowing me to keep the dignity of the Master.

Christ, I'm lying to myself in thinking she's the same as all the others. She's not. She's not like them. She's not like anyone.

"Allow me to serve you, Master," she says quietly, her lashes demurely lowered.

Again, she's offering what I already have and again, that should earn her a punishment. But for the first time in years, neither the Master nor the man want to give that to her. She's not being manipulative and she doesn't deserve the flicker of anger I feel that she's somehow managed to get under my guard. She's being genuine and honest, so how can I not give her honesty in return? Because I do want her to serve me.

"A scotch," I tell her. "No ice."

"Your will, Master," she replies.

13

Odette

I slip off the couch, unselfconscious of my nakedness, because why bother about it now? When he's seen all of me and touched most of me? I feel strangely light and... whole in a way I haven't been for two years.

I don't know why simply telling this man what happened to me and having him give me reassurance in return made me feel this way, but it did. It's as if him testing me and giving me a chance to prove myself was exactly what I needed. Who knew? But he's given me back a small piece of myself that I thought was lost, so now it's my turn to do something for him.

I go quickly over to the cabinet where he keeps his drinks and get out a new glass. Then I open the scotch, pour a careful measure into the tumbler, and turn back to him. He's sitting down on the couch, his elbows on his knees, his hands clasped loosely between them while he stares at the floor. His expression is like granite and yet...

After I'd come back down to earth from two shattering orgasms in succession, he was there beside me, running a warm cloth over me, lingering on all my sore and sensitive places. He didn't speak as he did so, but I could see something in his eyes change, a shadow passing through them. And without thinking, I opened my mouth to ask him what was wrong. He snapped at me then, and I had to apologize, appalled at myself for stepping out of line since he hadn't given me permission to speak. But then... he'd told me why he didn't do aftercare and it was because of his wife.

That had shocked me because I wasn't expecting him to say anything at all, let alone that. But I could hear the note of pain in his voice, could see it in his eyes too, dark shadows obscuring all the blue. And my heart had squeezed tight in my chest as a wave of sympathy for him caught at me.

I don't know what it's like to lose someone I love, but I know what it's like to grieve. When I lost my confidence, courage, and strength after the attack, I grieved for the life I should have had. I grieved for the loss of the person I was before it happened. It's not the same as losing a loved one and I know that, but still. I ached for him.

He's such a hard man, yet I could picture him caring for his wife the way he cared for me. Careful, gentle, methodical. Since he's a man who likes control, it must have been so difficult for him to have no way to save a person he loved. Maybe that's why he's so hard, why he must have complete command over everything, so he can feel he still has some power left.

It came to me then that we were very alike in a way, both of us experiencing an awful, random event that left us feeling powerless. He retreated into his work while I retreated from the world entirely, living like a hermit in my apartment.

I couldn't tell him that though, not when he'd not given me permission to speak, so I touched his cheekbone without even thinking about it, wanting only to give him some comfort. His gaze had flared at my touch, a complicated kind of heat moving in the shadows of his eyes and I wondered if he was going to punish me. But then he grabbed my wrist and held it, staring down at me, and for a moment I felt something wordless pass between us. Then some sixth sense told me that while he was the Master and in control, I could also protect him by looking away. So I did.

But I wanted to do more than that. I was tired of being the one who was always seeking comfort. I wanted to provide it for a change, and I wanted to provide it to him. He'd given me so much pleasure, given me my spirit back, and so I felt as if that was the least I could do for him.

I knew I was speaking out of turn as I offered to serve him and there was a moment where I thought he'd refuse. But he didn't and I sensed that it meant something to him that I offered. It meant something that he accepted too.

Carrying the tumbler over to the couch, I go to my knees in front of him, offering the glass. "Your drink, Master," I murmur.

He waits a beat before taking the tumbler from me, then sits back, taking a sip. I glance up at him from beneath my lashes, helplessly drawn by how the light accentuates the lines of his brow, cheekbones and jaw. He's so fucking hot, I literally can't deal. But it's not just about his looks. That tantalizing glimpse of the complex man behind the Master has me hungry for more. And I have to acknowledge that there's a depth to him that his son lacks and while that's probably only because of his life experience, I'm still fascinated.

I feel closer to him than I ever did to Luc, because this is a man who has endured things and I am a woman who has endured things too. Things that other people can't possibly understand, because it didn't happen to them. My friends who didn't know what to say to me after the attack, and who were puzzled about why I couldn't go out. Who couldn't see why I might have dropped out of college or didn't understand why I found being with strangers difficult.

They had never had their trust in the world betrayed the way I had and the distance between me and them got too vast, in the end. Even Lucas, for all that he lost his mother, found it hard to connect with me. Or maybe it was only that he found it hard to connect with himself. Not that Lucas matters to me now, not when his father is right there.

"You keep looking at me, sub," Mr. Fairfax says mildly. "I haven't given you permission."

Instantly I lower my lashes, but I can feel his gaze on me, pressing down. It makes me shiver all over. "Apologies, Master," I murmur, staring down at my knees.

A finger slides beneath my chin and he's tilting my head up, leaning forward to look at me. "What do you see?" he asks unexpectedly, his blue gaze searching. "What do you see that fascinates you so much?"

I swallow, unsure of how honest to be. Then again, honesty is what he wants so what can I do but give it to him? "This is going to sound strange," I say. "But when I look at you all I can think is how alike we are."

His eyes widen slightly. "Alike?"

I've surprised him and I'm pleased that I have. But I don't want to overstep. "I don't want to offend you, Master," I say.

He's silent a moment, still looking at me as if I'm something new and interesting he's never encountered before. "You won't offend me," he says at last. "I want to hear what you have to say, Odette."

The sound of my name makes me blink and I realize that his voice is gentler and he's not looking at me with the laser-like focus of the Master. He's reverted to himself, to being Mr. Fairfax, so I shift, sitting cross-legged in front of him instead of kneeling.

"We're alike in that we've both had random, terrible things happen to us," I say. "And I think... I think we're both still grieving the lives we should have had if those things hadn't happened."

He frowns slightly, his gaze still pinned to mine, and takes another sip of his scotch. "It's been years since I lost Gabrielle," he says after a moment. "And I have a different life now. I don't think of what could have been."

"Don't you?" I can't help but say. "Isn't that why you don't like doing aftercare?"

More shadows flicker through his blue eyes and he glances down at the scotch in his hand, staring at it as if he can see the secrets of the universe in it. "It's impossible to forget," he says as if to himself. "I thought if I stopped doing everything that reminded me of her, things would be easier."

I watch his handsome face, my chest tightening at the expression on it. "I thought if I shut out the world, the world couldn't get me," I say. "But the world doesn't care about getting me. It doesn't care about me at all. It just keeps passing me by like I don't exist."

He glances at me again, that same searching look on his face. "And you're letting it, aren't you?"

"So are you," I say and as soon as the words leave my

mouth, I know they're true. He *is* letting the world pass him by, in working so hard and in withdrawing from his son. Where else and who has he withdrawn from? I can't stop studying him, watching all those shadows in his eyes, and seeing beneath them something intense and hungry. He loved his wife, that's obvious, but now she's gone, where does all his love go? Who does he give it to? Or is he alone? Has that love turned on him and now it's eating him alive?

You know the answer to that.

Yes. I don't know how or why, but I do. He's alone and all that love is locked away inside him, and he's trying to control it, to press it all down and pretend he doesn't feel it. But he does, I know he does.

"Am I?" His voice neutral, but I can hear the note of weariness in it. "I'm okay with that, if so."

"Why?" I ask him straight out. "You're not the one who died."

It comes out more challenging than I meant it too, and Mr. Fairfax tenses. "What would you know about it?" he snaps, the weariness gone, only anger there now. "You don't know what you're talking about."

"I haven't lost anyone, it's true," I admit, not flinching from his gaze, because this feels important somehow. "But I know what kind of life I've been living for the last two years. I buried myself, Mr. Fairfax. I shut myself away because I was afraid, and that's not living. That's a living death. And it seems to me that you're doing the same thing."

Anger flickers in his eyes. "What makes you think that you know anything about me?"

"I only know what Luc told me and what I've seen of you tonight," I say levelly. "Tell me I'm wrong about you then."

I shouldn't be pushing him and I know that. It's really not my place since I'm only his son's ex-girlfriend and his sub for the evening, nothing more. Then again, who else does he have to challenge him? To ask him hard questions and talk to him about difficult subjects? Maybe he's right and I'm wrong. Maybe he's got a whole host of friends he talks to. Maybe I really don't know him and all this stuff about us being alike is just some shit I made up in my head.

He sits there in silence for a long moment, staring at me. Abruptly, he drains his glass and puts it down on the carpet next to me. Then he leans forward again and this time he reaches out and cups my cheek in one large, warm palm. "You're not wrong," he says quietly. "And don't call me Mr. Fairfax. My name is Gideon."

I shiver at his touch, then flush with pleasure at being given his actual name. "Gideon," I echo, unable to resist saying it. "You deserve a life, you know. You deserve to be happy."

"And you think I'm not?"

"Do you?" I want to lean into his hand, but I don't, not when I'm challenging him.

A breath escapes him and he gives my cheek a caress before sitting back in the couch again. "You know the answer to that already, I think."

I do, and he isn't, and something in me wants to change that. I want to give him some happiness, even if it's only a moment of it.

So I shift once again, coming onto my knees and lowering my lashes, my attention on my thighs. "Please, Master," I say. "Let me tend to you. Let me give you some relief."

14

Gideon

She's kneeling on the carpet in front of me with her attention down just like a good sub should. Her hair is mass of wild white-blonde curls down her back, her body is all pale, silky perfection, and my cock is getting hungry for more.

But my body can fucking deal with itself, because the conversation we just had has put me off-balance in way I can't remember being before. She was so sharp and the way she looked at me, the things she said, were so insightful that she literally took my breath away.

She should have no concept of who I am, not as a man, and yet what she said about us being alike and letting the world pass us by...

She's right.

Perhaps. I know I cut off a lot of friends after Gabrielle's death, burying myself in my work so I didn't have to deal with them. I let my son grieve without me because I couldn't handle his grief as well as my own, and that has left scars on us both. The only physical contact I have is purely sexual in nature, and only when I have direct control over the situation. And the conversation I've just had with my son's twenty-something-year-old ex-girlfriend is the most I've talked to anyone about Gabrielle's death in years.

She *is* right. I'm closed off and isolated and the world is passing me by, but that's by choice. I didn't want to deal with the world and so I didn't. I still don't, and yet I can't stop looking at her and wondering what it is about her that has me talking like this and thinking like this?

Why, out of all the subs I've had, is she the one who has managed to get under my guard? Is it because of what she said? That we're alike? That we're kindred spirits in that our spirits have been battered and bruised and want comfort in each other?

She's beautiful, no question, but as I keep thinking and keep discovering, there's more to her than beauty. She's submissive and yet she was challenging me now as if she hadn't been obeying me seconds before. And now she's back to being submissive again, offering to tend to me.

I do not, a rule, let subs serve me anything other than their bodies. I don't have them bring me food or drink, or undress me, or bathe me. I don't like how those things close the distance between me and a sub, especially when the serving is in a non-sexual way.

So I should say no to her. Get another toy from the coffee table, maybe the flogger, and whip her for her insolence. Deny her another orgasm then have her suck me off. Get the butt plug that's still in the box, that I decided was too much for her first night, and put it in her, work it until she's crying and then take her ass with my dick.

I should... But... I'm tired all of a sudden. I'm tired of all of this. Tired of the grief and pain, and the regrets I have over Lucas. Tired of the barren field that my life has somehow become. Tired of fighting myself and my susceptibility to this beautiful woman.

She's here, offering me what both the Master and the man want, and so why shouldn't I take it? What harm would it do? She wants to give me relief, and yes, I fucking want it. I fucking need it.

"Beautifully offered," I murmur. "Well done, sub."

She flushes, a pretty pink wave washing down her neck and over her lovely breasts. "Thank you, Master."

"Yes," I say. "Yes, sub. You can tend to me."

She looks up then, a startled, bright silver glance directly at me before looking back down again. Another thing I should punish her for since I didn't tell her to look at me. But I'm not going to punish her. I saw how badly she wants to serve me and how it both surprised and pleased her that I accepted her offer. I'm not immune to her desires, and she's been so good, so honest and open with me. So generous, too, smart and sharp, and challenging into the bargain. What she wants, I want, and I'm even thinking of letting her have free rein to please me however she wants, which is something I never give a sub.

But like I've thought once already, she's different. She's special. Tonight, she's gotten under my skin and I want her to stay there.

"How best can I serve you, Master?" she asks.

I lean forward again, cupping her cheek the way I did before, wanting to touch her, lifting her gaze back to mine again. "However you like, sub," I say.

She blushes again, heat flickering in her gaze, and I drop

my hand, sitting back on the couch. Looking at her, letting her know I'm waiting for her to make her move.

And she does.

Rising with grace from the floor, she bends over me, her fingers reaching for the buttons on my shirt, undoing them one by one. She's unhurried and careful, as if she wants to make this slow unbuttoning last, and I find myself wanting it to last, too.

I watch her as she does it, observing the finely drawn lines of her face, the pale brows and sharp nose, the full mouth and pointed chin. And then further down over her throat and collarbones, to the softness of her breasts and pink and pretty nipples. It's a leisurely journey I take as I look further, over her stomach and down between her parted thighs to where she's even pinker. And slick, and hot.

Her hands shake as she pulls my shirt out of its tuck at my waistband, undoing those last couple of buttons. And I know she likes the way I look at her. Which is good, because she is quite the beautiful sight.

She spreads my shirt open and then eases it off my shoulders. I've already undone the cuffs so when she pushes the sleeves down my arms, the fabric slides off readily enough. Once I'm shirtless, her hands drop to my belt and she fumbles a little with the buckle. I don't help her, since her light touches and shaking fingers are evidence of how badly I affect her, and I fucking love watching her deal with that. It's getting me hard.

Finally she unbuckles my belt, then undoes the button and zipper of my pants and spreads the fabric wide. There's no hiding how hard I am and since I've decided I'm not going to deny myself this time, I want her to know what her handiwork has done to me.

"What are you planning, sub?" I murmur, watching her

pink face as she stares down at my cock as it pushes hard against the fabric of my boxers. "You've got me all worked up which means you're going to have to fix the problem."

"Yes, Master," she says breathlessly, her fingers fluttering over the fabric as if she doesn't quite have the bravery to touch me.

I put her out of her misery, saying quietly, "I told you to serve me however you like, so there's no need to ask permission."

She sucks in a little breath and then her fingers are on me, tracing the hard line of my cock through the fabric of my underwear. It's a maddening touch, too light and gentle, but I don't push her. I want to see what this woman is going to do next. She's been nothing but surprises so far and I want to see what others she has in store for me.

I expect her to pull my dick out, but she doesn't. Instead, she kneels back on the floor and attends to my shoes, taking them off with my socks, one by one. Once that's done, she kneels upright and grabs the waistband of my pants, her gaze lowered. "Let me take these off for you, Master," she says.

So I help her slide my pants off and my underwear too until I'm sitting naked on the couch. It's not a situation I usually find myself in, in a scene. It's the sub who gets naked and only if they're very lucky do they even touch my bare skin, let alone see my entire body.

I have no problem with nakedness, it's the intimacy of it that I have issues with. And yet sitting here now, watching my sub look at me with her eyes wide and her mouth a pretty O of surprise and pleasure, I'm wondering if I've been doing myself out of a few things that could have been very erotic.

She kneels upright on the floor in front of the couch,

between my spread thighs, and then she leans forward and I expect her to go straight for my cock. But she doesn't. Placing a hand on either side of the couch cushions, she leans in and presses her mouth to my throat. Then she moves down, raining kisses onto my chest and abdomen.

They're light kisses, and gentle, and then she lifts her hands and begins to touch me with the same gentleness. I haven't been kissed like this nor touched like this in years, as if I'm a precious work of art and worth taking the time over and I can't believe how fucking incredible it feels.

I'm hard and getting harder, yet I don't want to rush her. She's sensual and delicious and her mouth on me feels too good. Her hands stroking my chest and the heat of her body as she leans forward between my thighs is intoxicating. The Master wants to play, to grab her head and force it down, push my cock into her mouth, but I hold back because the way she's touching me feels too good to deny.

She strokes my stomach, leaning forward to place her mouth on my skin and I lift an idle hand, winding my fingers into the white-blonde fall of her hair. It's soft and silky, and I stroke it, watching her mouth move lower and lower. The pale silk of it brushes against my bare thighs, the hot press of her lips moving even lower, and I find I don't want to put her mouth where it needs to be. I like this slow exploration of me. I like the soft noises she makes as her tongue licks the muscles of abdomen, a little hum, and the feel of her exploring fingers moving over my thighs.

Sensuality, yes, that's what this is. Unhurried. Easy. Touching for the sake of it, for the pleasure. I can't remember the last time I let a sub do this, and maybe I never have. Maybe I've never let a woman touch me this way, not since Gabrielle.

Her fingers stroke down my calves and then slide around

behind them and stroke back up, and a shiver goes through me. Fuck, since when do I shiver when a woman touches me? When usually it's the other way around?

But I don't want to stop her so I don't, letting her lick me, touch me, caress me. Then she lifts her head, her face pink, her silver eyes glowing like stars.

Fuck, she's beautiful.

"May I taste you, Master?" Her voice is husky and I can hear the hunger the words. Can see it in her eyes too, and I love that she's hungry for me. I fucking love it.

"Yes." I want that mouth of hers around my cock and I want it now, but I also want her gentle explorations, her little licks. My cock is hard, but my body is relaxed and I want to keep hold of that feeling. "But take your time."

She smiles at me then, as if I've given her a gift, and something in my chest tightens inexplicably. She was wasted on that son of mine, completely fucking wasted. He's too young, too full of himself, to truly understand what he had in her. He has the self-centeredness that young men do, not bothering to look beyond the end of their own dick because they're too caught up in what *they* want. Which is not a criticism — I was the same at his age. But I'm not now, and I can see the things he doesn't, such as her steel, her quiet courage, her glittering spirit. Her empathy.

She's breathing very fast as she touches my cock, stroking it gently with her fingers. Again, she's different. She's paying attention, being careful in a way I don't think another sub ever has, and it's maddening. I'm so fucking hard, my body impatient, but I don't want her to stop her delicate explorations.

She glances up at me, her silver gaze darkened now with desire, and even though she doesn't ask I know she wants to see if I'm okay with what she's doing.

Pretty little swan.

"Odette," I murmur, my voice rough with need, my fingers tangling gently in her hair. "The swan princess from Swan Lake."

Surprise crosses her face and then she flushes even pinker. "My mother named me after her. I don't much like it."

"Oh? Why's that?"

"Swans are supposed to be delicate and kind of breakable, and you know, the implications are..."

"Hate to break it to you but swans can be vicious." I smile at her as I wind a curl around her finger. I'm still hard as stone, but I can wait. I want to wait. "I had a couple in a pond in my house in the Hamptons. We had to give them a wide berth."

"Oh, well, maybe that's okay then," she says, grinning. "I don't mind being vicious."

"And they mate for life," I add.

Something flickers through her eyes, but it's gone before I can tell what it is. "I didn't know that."

"Well, now, you do." I meet her gaze. "Keep going, swan princess."

15

Odette

My heartbeat is all over the place and I can taste him on my skin. Salt and musk and a delicious flavor all his own. I've never taken my time over a man before, but kneeling before him, undressing him and then touching him is definitely up there in my top ten list of hottest things ever.

Now I've got his cock in my hand, long, thick, hard, and he feels so hot, his skin smooth and velvety. My mouth is watering and I want to taste him. He's given me permission, I'm clear on that, but this talk of swans has stuck in my head for some reason.

They mate for life...

The way he said that, the way his blue gaze held mine so steadily as if there was there was more— something hidden beneath the surface of the words that made my heart shudder in my chest. I thought Lucas might be the one for me — I'd even started thinking about us long-term before the attack happened — but I know now that he's not and he never was. I'm thinking about something else, some*one* else, and now he's put the thought in my head I can't get it out.

Maybe it's not Lucas who's the one for me.

Maybe it's him.

I lower my lashes as I lean in once again, dropping a kiss on Mr. Fairfax's hard stomach. His muscles tighten beneath my lips and when I kiss him lower, my fingers wrap around his cock and I feel his muscles tighten yet again.

There's a lump in my throat and I don't even know why it's there, because sure, I'm loving this encounter with this man, but I'm not falling for him. I hardly know him.

Except maybe you kind of do. He's got a wounded heart beneath that hard exterior and he's alone.

His fingers move in my hair, caressing it as I move my mouth lower, giving his magnificent cock a long, slow lick. His fingers tighten in reaction as I place my tongue on his skin, then they ease. I taste the salty flavor of him and it's delicious. I want more, so I lick my way around the blunt head of his dick.

I've got one hand on his thigh and I can feel the powerful muscles there tense in reaction. God, I love what I'm doing to him. I love how he tangles his fingers in my hair, stroking it as if he likes the feel of it in on his skin. And I love how kneeling here before him, knowing he's given me permission to touch his fucking amazing body anywhere, is the biggest thrill I've ever had.

But it's not just about his body. It's about the way he watched me as I undressed him, his blue gaze glittering from beneath his lowered lashes, and how, as I touched him, I felt his muscles relax, tension easing slowly from him.

Alone. Yes, he *is* alone. I can sense that in him and I can see it, because I'm alone too. I've been alone for years, trapped on the other side of an experience no one I know has ever had, and they can't imagine it. They can't cross that gap to where I am. He's like that too, he's trapped on the other side of his loss and no one can get to where he is, either.

It hurts me to think of him, stuck across that yawning void. It hurts me to think that's he alone. It hurts me to think that he lost a woman he loved and now she's gone, he's got no one at all. And he should have someone, he really should.

You maybe?

I shut my eyes, gripping his cock tighter and licking him again, giving myself over to the experience completely so I don't have that thought in my head. I don't want it there, because of course it can't be me. Not only am I so much younger than he is, I'm a college dropout with terrible anxiety issues. What would he ever see in me? What do I have to offer him? Besides, I'm not looking for another long-term relationship, not when I can barely manage my own bullshit let alone someone else's, and definitely not when he's my ex's dad.

I open my mouth and draw him in. He gives a deep, masculine growl of satisfaction as I do, which lights me up inside like candle. And I grip him tighter, moving my hand as I suck him, then licking him, nipping at him, glorying in his rich flavor.

"Fuck," he hisses. "You've got a hot mouth, sub."

The praise and the rough note in his voice makes me shiver in delight, and so I narrow my focus, taking him even deeper so the head of his cock is brushing the back of my throat, then sucking him hard. His hips shift as I do it, his fingers tightening in my hair, all the lazy relaxation in him gone as pleasure takes hold.

Lucas liked a blow job, except he always closed his eyes when I gave him one. Sometimes I used to wonder if he was imagining someone else rather than me, but I never had the courage to ask him. Mr. Fairfax, though, catches me beneath the chin and forces my head up so I have to meet his blue gaze.

"Watch me," he orders. "I want to see you swallow every fucking drop when I come."

The way he says that makes my whole body turn to flame. I couldn't look away from him if I tried. I'm lost in the dense blue of his gaze and suddenly all I want is to make him come and come hard. Give him the best blow job he's ever had. Suck him harder, take him deeper than anyone ever has, so he'll remember who did this to him. So he'll never forget me.

So I do and my eyes water as he thrusts into my mouth. But I can still see what I'm doing to him, how the pleasure burns like a flame in the blue of his eyes. And I see the moment he comes apart too, his face hardening and every line of him tensing. "*Fuck,*" he snarls. "*Jesus fucking Christ, sub.*"

Then he's coming hard, hot, salty liquid filling my mouth. And I'm swallowing him down, swallowing all of him just as he ordered me to, my own body shaking as much as his.

There's a moment of panting silence afterwards while I rest my head against his thigh. I can hear his breathing begin even out, his fingers idly tangling once more in my hair.

I close my eyes, my cheeks wet with tears from the brush of his cock against my throat, but also just.... from him.

From the thought of his loneliness. The thought of his grief and his pain, and the incredible loss he experienced. I don't know why it hurts me so much. I don't know why he matters, because he shouldn't. We're just having sex, not deep, heart-to-heart chats.

Mr. Fairfax lets out a breath and reaches down, pulling me up and into his lap. I'm facing him, my legs spread on other side of his lean waist. It's amazing sitting on him, both of us naked, skin to skin. His face is relaxed, the remains of the orgasm glowing in his eyes, and I want to touch the lines at the corner of his eyes, lines of experience, of pain and grief. There are lines around his mouth, too. It's so hard. He doesn't smile a lot, I can already tell, and that hurts me too.

"Magnificent, sub," he says, his voice roughened. "That was fucking magnificent."

His praise warms me all the way through until I'm glowing like a lightbulb. It's probably stupid to feel so pleased with myself, but I do. "Thank you, Master," I say. "And thank you for allowing me to care for you."

His blue gaze is hot and he's looking at me as if he's never seen anything like me before in his entire life. He's not so much a scientist now, wanting to dissect me, but a man looking at a lottery ticket and finding that all the numbers are winning ones.

I've never been looked at like that in my entire life.

He's silent a moment, then he says. "Why did you hide yourself away? Let the world pass you by?"

I shouldn't really be so surprised at how he keeps asking me unexpected questions and doing unexpected things, since he's been doing that all night. Yet somehow, I'm still shocked by the question. I'd thought he'd forgotten what I told him.

I'm unable to hold his gaze so I look down, trying to

think of the least pathetic answer, but then he takes my hands and places them on his chest, palms down. Beneath his hot, velvety skin, his muscles are rock hard and I feel the slow, steady beat of his heart. "Look at me, sub," he orders softly, covering my hands with his and holding them against his skin.

Reluctantly, I lift my lashes to look him in the eye. "I was afraid," I say simply. "I was afraid of everything and everyone. It was so dumb. I couldn't go to college, couldn't do anything but sit in my apartment with the door locked."

His hands over mine are warm, his chest against my palms hot. I love touching him. "Why do you say it's dumb?"

"I mean, it is, isn't it? My parents didn't understand what was wrong with me, how I could throw a Yale scholarship away like that just because of an assault. But they didn't understand." I swallow past the lump in my throat. "No one did."

He's quiet, just gazing at me. Then he says, "When Gabrielle died, I shut myself away. The only place I went to was the office, the only thing I concerned myself was work. I buried myself in it, cutting off friends, cutting off my son. You said that I wasn't the one who died, and you're right. I wasn't. But it felt like it for a long, long time."

"That's different," I begin. "You lost your—"

"And you lost your belief in yourself," he interrupts gently. "What I'm trying to say is that we both lost things that were important to us. Which doesn't make us dumb, only lost."

I don't know why those words hit me the way they do, like a cannonball to the foundations of my soul, shaking me. I stare into his blue eyes, seeing not the Dom, or Luc's father, or the CEO of a massive company. Seeing only the man, grieving, hurting, alone....

"I don't feel lost with you," I say before I can stop myself. "I don't feel afraid. With you, I feel found."

Something shifts in his eyes and it looks like regret, and I know immediately what he's going to say. He's going to remind me that this is only one night, that there can't be more than this, and I shouldn't get attached. But I have a horrible feeling it's too late for that for me, and I have to get these words out. I have to tell him so he knows. "And... I want to find you too, Gideon. You don't have to stay lost if you don't want to be."

The expression on his face shifts again, his blue gaze flickers, and I know I've said too much. He's going to say something now, perhaps send me away, and I can't bear it. I don't want to end it like this, so I lean forward and press my mouth to his.

He must know what I'm doing, yet he doesn't move, still holding my hands pressed to his chest. But he doesn't kiss me back, either, and it hurts. In fact, everything about this is suddenly exquisitely painful. I shouldn't have said anything. I've ruined the moment, been too open, been too-full on. So I do the only thing I can.

"Please Master," I whisper against his lips. "Let me choose another toy."

16

Gideon

She's distracting me, trying to hide her feelings from me, but I'm an old hand at this and I know what she's doing. I shouldn't have said anything about Gabrielle, shouldn't have shared that with her, yet I did. And now it's too late.

With you I feel found...

Fuck, the look in her eyes when she said that. She was... glowing, her whole soul in her gaze, and she let me see it. She held nothing back. And all I could think was that it's been such a long fucking time since I've made anyone feel anything beyond physical pleasure. A long time since I've made anyone feel anything beyond grief and pain.

You don't have to stay lost if you don't want to be...

Her mouth on mine is hot and desperate, and I know what she's trying to do. She said too much and now she's trying to distract me, and I should let her. Because she's starting to feel something for me and that isn't supposed to happen. I've had subs who did even though I told them I couldn't offer them anything more— these things can happen no matter how careful you are — and the situation always gets messy and painful in the end.

I don't want to hurt Odette, and I'm a fucking bastard for liking how I made her feel. For seeing the silver flame of her soul burning in her eyes as she told me I didn't have to stay lost if I didn't want to be. And it's such a beautiful, generous soul, too.

But there can be nothing between us. Not here, not with her. All I want is a sub for the night and that's all I'll ever want. I had a wife once and I loved her, but I'm a different man now, a harder man, a colder man. I won't ever be anyone's husband or partner again, and I don't want to be.

So I take her offer of distraction, pulling her hands from my chest and sliding her off my lap. I don't look at her, yet I can still feel the warmth of her hands against my skin, and it lingers like the heat from a burn.

I go over to the coffee table, looking down at the toys all laid out there.

I've been going easy on her so far, so perhaps now it's time to up the stakes, show her who she's really dealing with, make her see me for who I am. Which is not the grieving widower she needs to heal or *find,* but a cold, dominating bastard who'll push her unmercifully no matter how softly she looks at me.

That's a poor reward for what she's given you.

I ignore that thought. She gave me a great blow job, and now I'm going to blow her fucking mind. That's not a poor reward. That's why she's here.

After a moment's consideration, I note the lube I left in the box, then pick up the flogger. First a little light whipping, then I'll fuck her in the ass. It won't be what she's expecting, and it might be too much for her, but she's got her safe word. All she needs to do is say it and all of this will end, and she can leave.

You don't want it to end, though.

No, I don't. But it has to. For her sake.

I grit my teeth and turn back to her. She's sitting on the couch, watching me with big eyes that only get bigger when they see the flogger in my hand.

"Get up and bend over the arm of the couch," I order bluntly. "Quickly now."

There's no hesitation as she slips off the couch, going down to one end of it and laying herself gracefully over the arm. The rounded curve of her ass is in the air, her hair draping over the sofa fabric, her hands braced on the cushions.

I come to stand behind her, studying the arched bow of her body, noting the pink flesh I can see between her thighs and how wet she is. Giving me that blow job turned her on, and she hasn't had any relief, yet. Well, she won't be getting any relief soon either. I'll push her as hard as I can, get her to safe word out, then I'll let her go.

She's shivering with anticipation and when I gently trail the leather falls of the flogger over her back and ass, teasing her, she jerks.

She's so responsive. Finding another sub as honest and open and as beautifully reactive as her is going to be tough. But I'm sure there are plenty of subs out there who are. I just need to find them.

"This is going to hurt," I tell her. "But I think you can take it."

I begin slowly and gently, laying light strokes over the curve of her ass, going soft at first. She gasps and jerks at the first strike, but I don't give her time to process it, I bring the flogger down again and again, the falls hitting the same place, building the pain. She cries out, her body shaking, her ass getting pinker and pinker.

You can't punish her for telling you something you didn't want to hear.

Something in me tenses, but I try to ignore the thought. I'm not punishing her for telling me how I made her feel, that would make me a piss-poor fucking Dom. I'm pushing her, yes, but only to—

Make her safe word out? That makes you a piss-poor fucking Dom too.

I pause for a moment, ignoring the thought and ignoring, too, the tight feeling in my chest. I need to check her boundaries, that's all. This is about her, not me, it's *all* about her.

Furious with myself and trying not to be, I glance down at her face to check on her. She's got her cheek pressed to the couch cushion, her head turned to the side, and I catch the sheen of wetness on her pink skin.

Are these tears of pain and pleasure? Or are they from something more? Perhaps from me taking the distraction she offered after her confession? Me not giving her anything in return?

My chest is tight, a thread of self-loathing creeping through me. Fuck, I don't want her to cry, not over me. I'm not worth anyone's tears, especially not hers.

"You want to use your safe word?" I ask, my tone rougher than usual.

"No," she says, her voice a thready whisper that pierces my chest like a fucking arrow.

It's wrong of me to keep her here. It's just fucking wrong, especially given what she told me about how I make her feel. Especially when she's offering the same thing to me.

You don't have to stay lost...

My chest aches. She shouldn't be saying such things. She has no idea what she's offering. She has no idea how many times and ways a heart can break until it's shattered beyond repair. She knows nothing about anything, so why she should be saying this bullshit to me, I have no idea.

I stare down at her, trying to force away the feelings of anger and self-loathing. Trying to find the focused, hard strength of the Dom. "Don't fucking lie to me, sub," I growl.

She turns her head to the side, her cheek on the couch cushions, and her eyes meet mine. They're dark with arousal and yet there's pain there too. Physical yes, but it's more than that. I *know* it's more than that, because she's not looking at the Dom. She's looking at the man.

"I'm sorry," she says hoarsely. "I should never have said—"

"Don't," I interrupt, because I can't let her think it was her mistake. "You don't need to apologize. You did nothing wrong."

She blinks, tears sliding down her cheek and dripping onto the couch cushions.

"It's me who should be sorry," I add, unable to stop myself. "Because there's no way out, Odette, not for me. I have to stay lost."

"No you don't." Her gaze is level and I can see a fierce determination burning there, seeing all the way into me. "Not if you don't want to be."

I can't stand the way she's looking at me. It's like she can see past all the bullshit, see right into the heart of me.

See past all the lies you tell yourself.

I straighten, shoving the thought aside, gripping the

flogger once again. I bring it down on her backside a couple more times, trying to find my center, trying not to let the coiling, toxic mix of anger and self-loathing in my gut get the better of me. But I can't seem to find it. The cold, sharp focus of the Dom keeps slipping out of reach, which is dangerous.

Forcing myself to stand back, I let the flogger fall onto the floor.

She's panting, little sobs escaping her, but she doesn't move. Her ass is bright pink, the marks of the flogger standing out sharply against her paler skin, and between her thighs I can see how wet she is.

I don't know why she's letting me do this to her. I don't know why she won't leave. I can't give her what she wants and she knows that, and yet she's still here.

I move to stand beside her, looking down at her once again. She has her eyes closed, her lashes wet with tears, and the tight feeling in my chest tightens even more. "What the fuck are you doing, Odette?" I demand, unable to stop myself. "Say your fucking safe word."

Her eyes stay closed. "No."

There's no give in the word. It's hard, strong, determined. Just like her.

My jaw aches. The cold stone in my chest, the one that took the place of my heart, nudges its sharp edges against my ribs.

I don't feel lost with you...

Jesus, what did I do to make her feel like that? Pulled her hair, flogged her, put nipple clamps on her, made her beg. There's nothing about me that should have made her feel that way. Not one fucking thing.

You should send her away. Now.

I should, especially when I'm feeling like this. I should

be fully in control of myself, because it's dangerous if I'm not, and yet I can't bring myself to tell her she should leave. I need her to do it. I need her to say her safe word, to give me the excuse to send her away. And it's ironic that in the space of a few hours, the power balance has slowly tipped in her favor and I'm left with nothing.

Gritting my teeth, I pick the tube of lube out of the box before going back to the couch. She's draped over the arm, her pink ass in the air. I flick the cap off the tube and squeeze some of the cool gel onto my fingers. Then I slide my hand between her ass cheeks, finding her tight little asshole and easing a finger inside, spreading the lube around.

She jerks as my fingers touch her, then she gasps as my finger slides in and she's squirming around on the sofa arm, shuddering as I manage to stretch her a little. "I'm going to fuck your ass, sub," I say flatly, a current of rough heat in my voice. "And you'll take me, won't you? You'll take all of me."

"Y-Yes, Master," she says hoarsely, her whole body trembling.

"You can say your safe word." I work my finger deeper, leaning over the arm so I can watch her face as I do. "You know what it is?"

Her cheeks are scarlet now and wet with tears, but her darkened silver gaze is still blazing. "Yes," she says thickly. "I remember, Master."

But she's not going to say it, is she? I can the determination in her eyes and the certainty. She's not going to give it to me and I have no one to blame for that but myself. I was the one who demanded her trust and her surrender, and she gave them both to me.

You can't throw them away as if they mean nothing.

I shove the thought from my head, working her ass with

my finger, getting her nice and slippery in preparation. And she shivers and trembles, the sound of her soft moans filling the room.

I should send her away right now, especially since she's not going to give her safe word, but I'm hard and spreading all the lube around has gotten me even harder. So I'll take what I want first, get her off a couple of times as a nice reward, and only then will I send her away.

Coward.

A wave of anger crashes through my defenses. I'm not a coward, fuck that. Sending her away isn't about me, it's about her. She's not meant for me. She's meant for something better, some*one* better. A younger man who hasn't been tarnished and broken by loss. A man more honest with himself than I am, more adept at keeping relationships than I am. A man who hasn't burned his whole life to the ground due to grief.

I pull my finger out of her then reach to grip her hips, hauling them back so the soft, hot flesh of her ass is pressing against my groin. She feels so fucking good. I wanted a whole night to explore her, but after this I'll send her away. She won't like it, she might even fight me, but in the end she'll thank me.

"Brace yourself, sub," I say roughly. "I'm going to fuck you now."

17

Odette

I can feel him behind me, his hot skin against the backs of my thighs and my burning ass. There are tears on my cheeks and while some of them are from pain, not all of them are. Some are for me, for my cowardice in distracting him with yet more toys.

I didn't want to push him, didn't want to break the spell, and so I embraced the pain of the flogger, letting it hurt me and not even bracing myself for the blows— getting lost in the sensation so I didn't have to think any of my other stupid feelings.

But then he went and told me I didn't need to apologize for what I said, that I'd done nothing wrong, and the look in his blue eyes when he told me he had no choice but to stay lost... That was more painful than the flogger.

And it's why I won't give him my safe word, even though I know he wants me to say it. He wants an excuse to send me away, but I'm not going to give him one. He said he had to stay lost, but there was something else in his blue eyes when he said it. A kind of despair and fear. He's alone, but he doesn't want to be, I feel it in my soul, because if he did he would have sent me away immediately.

I'm not going to give him a reason, though. I'm going to stay as long as he'll allow it, because no matter what he says, he doesn't want to stay lost.

He wants to be found.

So I grit my teeth instead, my hands fisting in the couch cushions as I feel the head of his cock pressing against my ass and pushing inside, slowly, relentlessly. I can't stop the wail that escapes me and I press my hot face into the velvet of the sofa, moaning into the fabric. It hurts even with the lube, and that's mainly because he's so fucking big.

I never did this with Lucas, not once, and I'm fiercely glad we didn't. I want one thing that's just Gideon's and I guess my ass is it.

I can feel myself stretching around him and I groan, even as I arch my back so he can go deeper. It hurts like fuck, but I don't care. I want this. I want him. He reaches forward, closing his hand around my throat and the weight of it— like a steel collar around my neck— makes everything sharper, more intense. It's possessive, that hold, and I want to be possessed. I want him to possess me, every single part of me.

"You've got a tight ass, sub," he growls in my ear. "You ever had anyone fuck you there?"

"No," I gasp as he works even deeper. "No one. It's all yours, Master."

He says nothing to that, though his fingers tighten around my throat. Then I feel his other hand take my hip in a strong grip and I try not to tense up in anticipation. He moves, slowly at first then gathering speed, his hips thrusting and his cock pushing in and out of my ass.

It's agony. It's ecstasy. It's everything and I moan helplessly into the fabric of the couch.

"No," he says, his voice rough as gravel. "Let me hear it. I want every fucking scream, understand me?"

Helpless to do anything but obey, I turn my head to the side, my fingers holding on tight to the cushions for dear life, and I hold nothing back. I give him everything, every scream, every moan, every wail.

"Say it," he murmurs viciously in my ear, his voice so deep and rough its almost unrecognizable. "Say the word." He pulls out, then slams back in.

"No." The word breaks into a moan as he pulls out then thrusts again.

"*Say the fucking word, sub,*" he snarls, giving another savage thrust.

"*No,*" I scream into the couch cushions. "I'm not going to say the fucking word. I'm never going to say the fucking word, no matter how hard you fuck me."

He gives a growl of frustration, and moves deeper, harder, pushing me to the limit. He thinks he can force it from me, but he can't. Because he's taught me I'm stronger than I ever thought I was, and I'm not going to break.

I'm going to break him instead.

He pushes me and he pushes me, and it hurts, but there's a dirty, savage pleasure to it too. I throw myself into it, glorying in it, and when at last he lets go of my hip and slides one hand between my legs, finding my clit, I know I've won.

And I scream as the orgasm rolls over me, grinding me into dust.

Everything after that is a blur. I can feel him thrusting

hard and deep until he falls out of rhythm. Then his teeth sink into my shoulder, his roar of release vibrating against my skin.

We don't move for a long time after that. His weight is pressing me down into the arm of the couch, making it difficult to breathe, but I don't care. I like feeling how relaxed he is, how sated. Because I did that to him. That was all me.

Eventually, he shifts, pulling out of me. And I feel him run light fingers down my spine, making me shiver. "Are you okay?" he asks, an edge in his voice. "Any pain anywhere?"

My ass is burning from the flogger and from his massive cock, but I feel as if I'm flying so it doesn't bother me. "No," I mumble against the fabric of the sofa. "Also, if you send me away now, I'm not going to go. You'll have to call the police to have me arrested for trespassing."

There's a long silence. Every muscle of my body is lax and honestly, I don't think I can move. My legs are jelly and my arms are noodles. I'm just going to collapse in a gelatinous heap on the carpet.

Except then I feel his arms around me, gathering me up. And somehow I'm lying against his hot, bare chest and we're moving. My head is resting against his powerful shoulder and when I look up at him, there's a strange expression on his face. I can't work it out. "You heard what I said, right?" I ask. "I'm not leaving."

He glances down at me, a flash of intense blue. "You should have said your safe word."

"Why? I didn't say it, because I didn't feel unsafe."

A strange expression flickers over his face. "You should have."

His shoulder is warm, the muscle beneath his skin powerful and solid. I'm feeling good, so good. Good enough that I say, "Don't do that, Gideon."

"Don't do what?"

"Don't distance me."

"You're a fine one to talk," he says. "Using toys to distract me."

"You didn't have let yourself be distracted," I point out.

He doesn't reply, carrying me down a short hallway before turning and going into a huge bathroom. Setting me on the vanity top, he goes over to a massive walk-in shower and turns it on, holding out a hand to test the water. Then, when he's satisfied with the temperature, he comes over to me, picks me up again, and then steps into the shower with me in his arms. The warm water is heaven and I close my eyes as he sets me on my feet. His hands move over my body as he washes me with the most incredible-smelling body wash. I feel as if I'm floating and I don't want to come down, especially when he moves under the water with me and I'm held against his muscled chest, his fingers moving up and down my spine.

"Jesus Christ, what am I going to do with you?" he asks softly.

I open my eyes and look up at him, the water falling around us. His eyes are the most brilliant shade of blue. "You're going to keep me," I say. "I'm going to be your sub. And one day, when you're ready, I'll come and find you, and you won't be lost anymore."

He doesn't look away. His dark brows draw down in a slight frown, yet his arms around me tighten. "You can't fall for me, Odette. I'm twice your age, I'm grieving, I've got nothing to offer anyone right now, let alone one young woman who deserves far more than I can give her."

"Too late," I say, because it *is* too late. I've fallen for him already and I know it. "Besides, how do you know what I deserve?" I lay my palms on his broad chest, feeling the heat of his body burning into my skin. "Perhaps a man twice my age and grieving, with nothing to offer, is exactly what I deserve."

His gaze holds mine and I can see desire flicker in the blue depths, along with a hunger for something else, something more. "Odette," he says again, and I can hear the regret in it. But not only regret. I can hear longing in it too.

"Well," I say. "I'm not going to force myself on you if you don't want it." And I try to step away. It's a gamble doing this, because he might indeed let me go, and I don't know what I'll do if he does. Yet just when I think his arms are going to open, they tighten instead, pressing me for firmly against his body. "No," he says, his voice deep and rough. "Don't go."

I stand very still, looking up at him, my heartbeat racing. "You want me to stay with you?"

His eyes are a fierce, dense blue. "Yes," he says. "No. Fuck, I don't know."

I lift an eyebrow as a warmth fills me that has nothing to do with the temperature of the water. "How about I stay for a little bit longer. The whole night, say."

He's looking at me with a fierce intensity now and there's a kind of awe in it, too. "Tomorrow night, too," he says.

"Okay." I lean against him and smile, feeling as if I've just been given a winning lottery ticket. "I'll check my diary but I don't think I've got anything on."

His hands lift and he cups my face between his large, warm hands, the look in his eyes searching. "You know I have nothing to give you, right? You heard that? I'm twice your age, my heart is fucking dead, and I have no idea how to be in a relationship with anyone let alone you."

I relax against him, his body hard and hot and strong, the feeling in my heart sinking deeper and deeper, and I don't resist. I surrender, because I've learned how. And maybe in time, I can teach him to surrender too. "I don't care." I look up at him, straight into his beautiful blue eyes. "I'm an anxious mess who overthinks everything, so I guess we're even."

"Odette," he says again, a little helplessly, his thumbs stroking along my cheekbones.

"It's okay," I whisper. "I'm staying."

He looks down at me a long moment, and then slowly, but surely, his mouth curves. It's a faint smile, but it's very definitely a smile, and right then and there I swear to myself that I'll make him do it again and again. "Tonight," he says. "Stay tonight and tomorrow. And then we'll see where we are."

Then he bends and kisses me and then it's my turn to smile, because I know exactly where we'll be.

Together.

EPILOGUE

Gideon

That one night became two, then three, and then a week passed, then six months, then a year, and she's still here. Every so often she'll check with me that it's still okay for her to stay and every time she asks, I answer through my teeth, "If you ever fucking leave, I'll drag you back here myself."

After three months, I came home to find my penthouse full of little knickknacks and pillows and sculptures and all sorts of other female paraphernalia. Apparently, she'd moved all her stuff in when I wasn't looking, and so I had to punish her. Naturally we both enjoyed it immensely, though I didn't tell her to move any of her things out. I was starting to like the pillows, anyway.

I've tried to repair my relationship with Lucas and while we're getting there, it's going to take some time. I told him flat-out about Odette, that we were together, and he was at first furious with me. Not because he wanted her, but because he thought I was taking advantage of her. She soon put him straight, since she's no one's helpless victim, and now he's coming round to the idea.

She's an obedient little sub when I'm her Master, but when we're Gideon and Odette, she argues and fights with all the stubborn determination in her soul. She's magnificent. She's perfect. She's everything I wasn't looking for and didn't know I needed, and I have a horrible feeling that I'm falling in love with her.

Or maybe I've already fallen. Maybe I fell that first night in the hotel room, when I turned around saw her standing there.

One thing I'm certain of though, is that before, I was lost and now, I'm found.

My swan princess found me.

Enjoy this?
Try the other books in the Lessons in Dominance Series!

After Hours by Caitlin Crews
Bad Girl Dilemma by Zara Cox
Bound and Branded by Maisey Yates

ABOUT JACKIE

Jackie writes dark, emotional stories with alpha heroes who've just got the world to their liking only to have it blown wide apart by their kick-ass heroines.

    She lives in Auckland, New Zealand. When she's not torturing alpha males and their gutsy heroines, she can be found drinking vodka martinis, reading anything she can lay her hands on, wasting time on social media, or knitting yet more sweaters she doesn't need.

www.jackieashenden.com

facebook.com/HouseofAshenden
instagram.com/jackie_ashenden

EXCERPT FROM AFTER HOURS BY CAITLIN CREWS

I

He was there again that night, like something the dusk called up from the bay and let loose upon the gritty, crumbling city.

Calamitous villain or savior, it was hard to tell.

The man was built like some kind of modern day Viking, what with the dark beard and those icy blue eyes. He was also one of those sculpted, muscled, *huge* men her ex-husband had liked to sneer at and call *CrossFit junkies* like that was something to be embarrassed about when *he* had liked to prance around in a lot of cycling apparel while doing very little actual cycling.

Though Joseph had known better than to sneer about anything where any of those much larger men could hear him, of course.

Romily had seen the man before. Her latter day Viking. She had made a point of it, in fact.

Her little hideaway-from-the-whole-world boat was docked in a small, weathered marina near Brooklyn Basin in

Oakland, and there were only a handful of places in the area that weren't entirely overcome by the relentless press of the streets.

Some called even that little bit of so-called civilization gentrification, which they meant as an insult. Personally, Romily liked not getting shot at when she needed a few things from the self-consciously precious little market nearby. It existed solely to cater to the fancy new high rises in the Brooklyn Basin development, all boasting some of the most beautiful views imaginable of San Francisco across the water at astronomically high prices. She even liked the absurdly uppity prices at the market—the *fact* of them, the optimism they suggested about the clientele, not actually *paying* them—and that the little boutique grocery had about seventy-five varieties of Boba, every alternative milk imaginable, and yet shockingly few actual necessities. She liked the strangeness of this new life of hers more and more—or so she told herself daily, like a mantra— so far away from what her small and claustrophobic life in Walnut Creek had become. Walnut Creek, which never had been as close to San Francisco as the people who lived there liked to pretend, and where Joseph had made certain that any friends she might have had lost touch with her completely.

He'd made certain of it but she also hadn't fought it, because surrendering to her ever-increasing isolation was easier than explaining why she was the way she had to be to survive him.

The market was one of the surprising rewards she'd found for making an entire new life for herself, unconnected to anyone or anything she'd known before, in a place no one who'd ever met her would think to look for her.

Another was *him*. The man.

Her bearded, mouthwateringly well-cut Viking who was

usually in what she'd originally thought was a garage, thanks to its roll-up metal door covered with the expected spray-painted tags. It sat between a bizarre sort of down market seafood restaurant that did a surprising amount of business, given the often questionable neighborhood there on the Embarcadero, and a seedy though not wholly terrifying dive bar. The bar came alive only late at night and often left its patrons worse for wear as well as targets for petty thieves as they stumbled off along the waterfront path that stretched all the way to Jack London Square.

And it turned out it wasn't a garage. Romily had found that out one very early morning when she couldn't sleep and so was out walking. An activity that was not as relaxing as she'd hoped, given what lurked in the shadows beneath the palm trees here, but it was a lot better than her nightmares.

She'd heard the noise before she'd understood what she was hearing, odd metallic crashes and a kind of growling through the morning fog, making her wonder if she'd been about to encounter another monster she would have to run from.

Or, more worryingly, if maybe it was time she ran *toward* the monster instead, because there was something almost exhilarating in the thought of *choosing* it—

But there were no monsters. Not the kind that chased her, anyway.

It was a gym.

One of those gyms with black floors and horrible, shouty music, filled with terrifying equipment like bags hanging from chains like some kind of fitness abattoir— without a single soothing elliptical machine or smoothie counter to be seen.

What it had was *him*.

Sometimes other big, scary men were there too. They all looked like they were trying to make themselves into his clones, but never quite got there. There were a lot of bearded, tattooed, grim-eyed men in that dark little place, all crashing weights and grunting noises, but only *he* seemed to disturb the air when he moved.

And that was hard to do in this part of Oakland, where *disturbance* was just regular, daily background noise.

Those disturbances were why Romily didn't love leaving her boat. Well. One reason, anyway. If she could, she'd stay hidden away in the marina night and day, but even someone who wanted to stay anonymous and forever unfound had to go out sometimes.

So every day, Romily made herself leave the marina and walk around, because that was what people were supposed to do, and she was trying her best to do that. To *people* like she really was a person and not just the ruined, bombed-out shell of a person her ex had made her.

And not only when the nightmares had her waking up choking again.

After that first morning, in the fog, she'd made it a point to learn the hours of the gym—and they weren't posted anywhere she could see. Apparently you had to have a beard and a certain grimness to you to work it out.

Or you had to live nearby, like Romily.

By now she had managed to see him at almost all times of day.

There was usually a t-shirt situation but on really good days, he was shirtless. Curling things. Slamming things. Sometimes running with all his sleek muscles on display, not to mention the kind of tattoos that had always fascinated her, all over his skin like spells and incantations. Sometimes at night she would lie in her berth and trace the patterns she saw inked into his skin all over her own body.

Sometimes she would slide her hands between her legs and let her imagination go wild—

Tonight, though, he surprised her.

Shocked her, even.

Because tonight she saw him when she hadn't expected it. When she wasn't looking for him, for a change.

He was walking out on the commons—the public park behind the old Port of Oakland building that offered dreamy views over the estuary and further on toward San Francisco. He was just *there,* like he wasn't a gorgeous, terrifying warrior of a man, out in the falling dusk. As if he was *normal* instead of *extraordinary,* out here in public surrounded by regular people, and Romily didn't know what to do with herself.

She barely knew who she was. She almost swallowed her own tongue. She was certainly holding her breath.

She froze, right in the middle of a stream of people, which was a good way to get trampled.

But she couldn't move.

It was a small miracle that there was a knot of skateboarders between them. Not that he would recognize her. Why would he? But she was sure he'd notice someone frozen solid and *gaping* at him.

It was a kind of miracle to see him like this. Just… out.

No crashing weights or music ripe with full-throated bellows and dark, hot baselines designed to disturb.

Just a powerfully built man prowling his way down a walkway.

He was mesmerizing.

He wasn't wearing the things he usually did in the gym. He was in jeans that made a grand feast out of the powerful muscles of his quads and ass. He wore a black Henley that only emphasized his outrageously cut arms. He wore a dark knitted beanie like every other bearded dude in the East Bay, but he was nothing like any of *them*.

Something about *him* made her bones hum and her body ache.

Like a good fever, if that was a thing.

Long after he'd walked off, back to whatever life he must lead and she should probably wonder about that at some point, Romily stayed frozen still. She didn't move even when the skateboarders looped all around her like she was a new obstacle for them to conquer.

She didn't move for so long that when she did, she felt stiff and something like sore.

In her chest, where the heart she'd written off as defective suddenly decided to start beating again, too hard and too jagged.

Hours later, instead of walking straight to the marina entrance and hurrying down the dock to the safety of her boat, she looped around on the walkway instead. She told herself she was simply enjoying a nightly walk—not something she normally indulged in this far from dawn, not least because it could get a bit nutty out here in the dark— but that wasn't entirely true.

Romily was deliberately taking another pass near the gym.

Just in case, she told herself.

Just in case what? she asked herself a bit scornfully. *He's standing around outside a gym on a Friday night? Just to see if he can cause a commotion?*

Not likely.

When she headed toward his gym, she saw that the garage door was closed. Not a surprise.

That there was a light on inside, though, was. She could see it through the cracks in the small, barred windows in the rolling garage door. Just a hint of light, peeking out into the dark.

Romily wasn't usually out this late, or for so long, but a lot of other people were because it was a Friday. And the weather was beautiful. There had been fleets of kayaks in the estuary all day. The restaurant was packed and loud. There were even people waiting in line to get into the dive bar.

She had gone out tonight as a test. There'd been music in the park, so she'd gone over to listen. Once she'd *unstuck* herself that was. She'd watched people dance. Sing. Roller blade through the evening. She'd made herself sit there in a crowd, like normal people did, even in this part of beleaguered Oakland.

But all the while she'd daydreamed about *him.*

Now she wanted nothing but to get to her boat and hide away again, so she could lie in her cozy berth and go over every detail of his pecs straining beneath that Henley, then make up some delicious scenarios to go with it, but that light taunted her.

Romily made her way past the crowd outside the bar, then did something she'd never done before. She didn't overthink it. She had a crazy little idea and she went with it. Instead of walking her usual path past the front of the gym and on to the marina's gated entrance, she slipped into the alley between it and the bar.

She felt breathless. Audacious.

Like the girl she'd almost been before Joseph had gotten his hooks in her.

Thinking about Joseph was galvanizing, because he would hate this. All of this. That she was in this part of

Oakland. That she lived on a boat of questionable seaworthiness. That she was having *whole thoughts and a life* without his permission and direction.

Not to mention that she noticed other men at all, much less one who looked like a Viking god.

He would make her pay for all of that. She knew that all too well. She'd lived it for longer than she liked to think about—

But Joseph wasn't here.

So Romily walked faster and with more determination into the dark, until the shadows swallowed her up.

And when she got farther still, she saw that there were stairs that led up to a higher floor above the gym. But beneath it was another door, with an actual name on it: *LONDON'S*. With a list of hours and a phone number etched beneath.

Like it was a real gym after all, not just a home away from home for Vikings lost in time.

But Romily didn't care about any of that, not at the moment, because she could see through the glass.

He was there. Right there, in what looked like some kind of front desk area, though she could barely concentrate on the details.

Because he wasn't doing paperwork.

He had a blonde woman bent over that desk and he was fucking her.

Hard.

Get it here:

After Hours by Caitlin Crews

EXCERPT FROM BAD GIRL DILEMMA BY ZARA COX

Chapter One

Dahlia

Not gonna lie, this is my favourite part.

Okay, maybe not my *absolute* favourite.

But watching pollsters on my heavily encrypted social media app lose their minds always gives me a buzz.

I watch two contenders battle it out until it hits the 85% mark, then the fickle public, as they always do, rally behind one.

Tonight's clear winner hits 92% and I grin.

Obsidian Corp it is.

I don't use the actual entity names beforehand of course because that would stupid. Obsidian is only known as DDD to my pollsters.

Lying on my stomach in bed, legs tangled in my sheets, chin propped on one hand, I wait for the stragglers to get on board. I like to get as close to 100% as I can.

There's a delayed gratification to that, a sizzling in my veins that comes with righteous sinning that's a high I like to skate as long as possible. Forget drugs, it comes as close to sex as I can get.

So while the disgruntled few whose initial picks didn't make the cut make up their minds, I swipe lazily across the screen.

The poll numbers spike in real time. Thousands of anonymous voices, weighing in on who deserves a taste of my justice.

My fingers hover over the voting breakdown.

Each name on the list makes my blood boil.

✦ A billionaire hedge fund vampire who crashed a housing market for sport.

✦ A pharmaceutical exec who jacked insulin prices mid-pandemic and is still at it.

✦ A prince with offshore accounts full of human trafficking money.

✦ DDD, founder of "O" Corp, crypto king, rumoured sadist, silent investor in all the above.

The comments under his name are extra spicy.

"That DDD guy gives me the creeps."

"Didn't he blackmail a journalist into disappearing?"

"Such a shame he's fuck-hot. Or is it??!"

"Do him and I'll tattoo your name on my ass."

I chuckle. My followers are feral, and I love them for it.

I'm no saint. I've never claimed to be. But there's something delicious about righteous vengeance dressed in latex and filtered through a voice modulator. I steal. I expose. I redistribute. I livestream it all. And if I get a little thrill watching corrupt assholes rage and lose their minds as they promise to hunt me down and "insert extremely unimaginative punishment of choice here"—also, dream on, fuckers—? *Bonus*.

When I hit 96%, I flip onto my back, flick out of the poll and swipe to another app. Just to...peek. I may be putting the proverbial cart before the horse but I'm already dreaming up ways to reward myself once I'm done notching another win under my belt.

The Club app opens in full dark mode, purring like a secret lover.

It was a joke at first—signing up. A little curiosity, a little mischief. I never expected to keep it. But somehow, logging on after a job has become a ritual, although tonight I'm doing it before not after. Which, if I believed in superstition, I would be fucked. But I don't so...

I don't talk much on the app. Just... watch. Explore. I've interacted a couple of times, but mostly I've created dirty little fantasies in my head I secretly hope will come true.

Dominants, subs, contracts, scenes.

Intimacy without strings.

Pain twisted into pleasure.

There's something almost reverent about it. Like control isn't something you seize—but something you surrender.

Maybe after this job, I'll finally do what I've been too chicken to do so far and...indulge. Dip my toe in the water, so to speak. I don't know how far I'll get because all that surrendering sounds copasetic in theory but yeah...I'm not the surrendering type.

Maybe a clean, anonymous hookup. No feelings. Just breathless, beautiful pain. A reward for a job well done. I scan a few profiles, half-distracted. A masked man with a wicked mouth. That Dom with blood-red leather gloves. The one I keep returning to over and over.

My pulse flutters. I take a note of his name.

SinMadeFlesh. Meh, not exactly original but whatever.

Maybe I'll message him. Later.

I shut down the app and return to the poll.

98%. That's as good as I'm going to get.

I roll off the bed, energy spiking as the prospect of vengeance.

Showtime.

###

My gear is already laid out: matte black cargo pants, tight turtleneck, harness strapped with micro-tools, soundless boots. My gloves are fingerprint-resistant, and my mask —sleek and mirrored—covers half my face, voice modulator built into the jawline.

I secure my ponytail, zip everything up, and look at myself in the mirror.

No one would guess I'm twenty-two. That I'm very partial to cereal for dinner and cry during Pixar shorts. That I once built a server farm in my mom's garage to DDOS a revenge porn site.

All they see is Spectre—digital thief, vigilante brat, chaos in motion.

Not Dahlia Wynn, cyber security expert and programmer.

I tap the go-live button. "Spectre, online."

My voice comes out distorted, laced with static and steel. The screen flashes green. My viewers spike fast.

"Yessss she's back."

"This one's gonna be juicy, I can feel it."

"Who's tonight's victim, Spectre?"

"You voted. I listened. It's Triple D," I purr. "Let's rob the devil."

###

The building looms like a monolith, all obsidian glass and silent menace like it's owner, reflecting the city like it's daring it to come closer.

I slip inside like smoke—through a service entrance, past sleeping cameras, under the pulse of motion sensors I've already looped. My custom drone buzzes softly at my side, flashing green when the path is clear.

Heart rate steady. Breathing controlled. No fear. I'm in the zone.

Until the actual heist, all I'll be charged with on the *extreme off chance* I'm caught is corporate trespassing. A slap on the wrist or a fine or some community service. Totally worth it. But I don't plan on getting caught.

Obsidian has the honour of being my introduction into double-digit heisting and I've been doing this for two years.

Up ten floors. Through the server vault. Past biometric locks. My custom key slips into the panel and I wait for the soft chime of access granted.

Ding.

I grin under the mask. Too fucking easy.

I plug in, fingers flying, siphoning encrypted data through my proxy chains, dumping it into blockchain wallets faster than a heartbeat.

The stream's eating it up. Comments fly.

"Holy shit, she's in."

"That's Triple D's master key, isn't it??"

"Fuck, five mil. Six! Gah, seven and a half!"

"You're on fire, Spec! Get it, girl!"

"GET OUT GET OUT—"

Wait. Something's wrong.

The files... they're looping. Duplicating. I blink.

INTRUSION DETECTED. TRACE IN PROGRESS.

Reverse beacon triggered.

User: SPECTRE

Location: LOGGED

Protocol: Velvet Vice Fingerprint Activated.

Cold drips into my veins. My drone flashes red.

What. The. Fuck.

No.

My breath strangles in my throat. I yank the drive, slam my laptop closed, kill the stream.

How did he—?

I've barely been here five minutes. To react this fast he'd have to have known. Have to have been lying in wait.

How the *fuck* did he know? Every piece of equipment I use is encrypted. Designed by me because I trust no one else in this world. Life lessons learned the hard way.

A voice slides through the earpiece. Not mine. Not filtered. Smooth. Male. Lethal.

"You shouldn't have been so sloppy, little thief."

I freeze.

There's no fucking way. I wasn't sloppy. I fucking wasn't.

The voice continues, low and wicked, right in my skull. "But I'm glad you were. I've been waiting for you."

Get it here:

Bad Girl Dilemma by Zara Cox

EXCERPT FROM BOUND AND BRANDED BY MAISEY YATES

Chapter One

Avery

There are two things that I'm certain of. The first is that every morning, no matter how tired I am the sun is going to rise in the east, and I'm going to have to get my ass out of bed to do the chores.

The second is that I *hate* Caleb Flynn.

I'm not exaggerating. It isn't mild dislike. It's the real deal. I *burn* with it. He's my nemesis, and has been ever since he bought that big plot of land next to ours. Ever since he built that giant, ostentatious house that stands on top of the mountain looking down on us like we're peasants, and he's the king.

Though, to him, I suppose that's the reality.

I don't like change, and the first strike against him was

that he changed my daily view. No longer do I look up and see the unadulterated mountains, but I also see his monstrosity of a house.

It's a beautiful house, but that's not the point. It's *different*. I get to hate it.

The second strike against him was when he bought up one hundred acres of our property. He made my dad an offer he couldn't refuse, and my dad took it. I'm mad at my dad about it, too, don't worry.

I'm fair with my hatred.

At least, I like to think so.

Since he bought up that hundred acres five years ago, he's also bought fifty more. I'm struggling to keep things going while dad refuses to give me total control, and this guy looming about all the time isn't helping.

So when I come into the house at dinnertime, and he's there, the acid churn in my stomach doesn't surprise me. Doesn't even disturb me. It's all the other feelings.

Because the problem is, even though I hate Caleb Flynn from the top of his cowboy hat down to the soles of his cowboy boots, he's also as hot as the fires of the hell that I would like to send him to.

It doesn't make any logical sense. It never has. I blame that night all those years ago. He did something to me. Changed something. Something I didn't want changed.

As far as my daily life goes, I want to be in charge.

No, I *need* to be in charge.

For as long as I can remember, control has the most important thing in my life. Mainly because neither of my parents has any. I love my dad, but without me, the ranch would've fallen apart a long time ago.

Caleb leases the land he bought back to us, and he thinks that gives him the right to come here when he wants to, to weigh in on our ranching practices and in general be around when I think he has no business being.

Caleb is... Well, he's the kind of man who thinks he's in charge of everything. He's the kind of man who thinks that the sun rises and sets on his word. No. It's going to do that regardless. One of those certainties.

Just like I'm going to keep on hating him.

"What are you doing here?" I ask.

As soon as the words exit my mouth, my dad comes in from the kitchen with two beers in his hand.

"Avery," he says. "Mr. Flynn is our guest."

I make direct eye contact with *Mr. Flynn*, those blue eyes scorching me. "Is that a fact?"

"It is," my dad says, sitting heavily in the chair next to Caleb, handing him a beer. Caleb looks at me meaningfully as he takes a long pull from the bottle.

"I'll have the papers for you to sign by tomorrow," Caleb says.

"No," I say, the word exploding from my mouth. "No. You're not selling him more of our land."

"Avery..." My dad sounds exhausted, but how the fuck does he think I feel? I'm the one who runs this place. I'm the one who makes sure that we have a ranch. I manage our ranch hands, and I keep up with the business aspects of it. I oversee the birthing, raising and slaughtering of the cattle, the selling of all the meat, this is mine. My blood, my sweat, my tears, and he's been parceling the ranch out to Caleb for years.

He might not be a property developer, but as far as I'm concerned, he might as well be. He's a rhinestone cowboy if anything. Just a rich dickhead who's doing this because he can. Buying up land and not even working it.

And what's the point of that?

I'm about to say exactly that when he stands. "We'll talk more tomorrow."

He looks at me, just for a second, and everywhere his gaze touches, I burn. With fury, with something else. But it's like I can't move. Like he's immobilized me with just his glance. I hate that too.

"What are you doing?" I ask.

"Business. With your father."

He walks past me like I'm an incidental. Like I don't matter. Like my feelings mean nothing. But I suppose to him my feelings don't mean a damn thing.

He walks out the front door, and I go after him.

I can hear my father's voice as I slam the door shut. No. He doesn't get to tell me what to do, not when I have to do everything. He doesn't get to exercise authority when he feels like it. Not when he can't keep the place stable without me.

"What's going on? I have a right to know. My dad's name might be on this land, but I'm the one running it."

He stops then and I keep going, bringing me almost toe to toe with him, and I can barely breathe. He's stunning, that's the problem. So tall and broad, his hair dark and though I've rarely seen him without a hat, I know it curls just a bit at the top and around his collar. His eyes are a piercing blue I can feel all the way through my body.

He's not quick with a smile, his mouth is grim, dark stubble covers his square jaw. He's more than classically handsome. It's almost enraging. Why should one man get wealth, strength, height and looks so fine they could topple mountains?

I'm short, poor, with hard won strength in my bony arms and deeply average breasts, which as far as I'm aware is the main feature men look at – unless they're into asses. As far as your face goes, if you're competent with makeup the glitter and flash seems to read as 'beautiful' to them no matter how your features are actually arranged.

I'm bad with makeup.

And I had one man who seemed totally fine with all that and I tanked that relationship.

Caleb Flynn remains tall, gorgeous and in my grill.

"I'm aware," he says, his gaze assessing. "Avery, you might not know anything about me, but I know everything about you. Everything about this ranch. I know what financial state you're in."

"I know that we burn through a lot of money –"

"No, you burn through money you don't have. I don't think you know how bad it is. Do you know how much your dad gambles?"

The words are like a slap. "Some."

"He's an addict."

"He's not an addict. He just… Likes to blow off a little steam."

"Avery, you're in danger of not ever having a shred of this ranch without my intervention. Luckily, I'm stepping in."

"Excuse me?"

"Your dad is borrowing money from me, but he's using the ranch as collateral."

"Are you… Are you kidding me?"

"No. I'm not."

"This is our land. You… You're a predatory son of a bitch. You've been buying off chunks of this property ever since you moved in, and this is what you've been waiting for."

"What the fuck do you think will happen if I don't intervene?" He asks, moving toward me, and I'm reminded of just how big he is. Broad, like the side of a mountain. Well over six feet.

"I don't..."

"Of course not, because you still trust him."

I scowl. "He's my father. I know he's not good with money, but I do a good job of managing this place, and we have enough."

"You don't," he says. "You, Avery Carmichael, are fucked."

The words are hard, crude and unforgiving and I find myself having to tamp down my physical reaction to them.

"Explain," I say.

"He owes people a lot of money and he hasn't been paying your mortgage. You're one more bad bet away from losing this place entirely and not to me, to people who will put you out on the street."

I feel the blood drain from my face. "That's not true."

"It is." He laughs. "You like to think of me as a villain, but have you forgotten that I let you off the hook when you tried to burn my barn down?"

The one bad thing I ever did and he has to throw it back in my face, and try to make me grateful for it.

"I haven't forgotten that you deserved it," I say.

"I could've called the police on you."

"You're welcome to do it now. I'll confess."

"No thanks. I don't have the appetite for it."

"Are you trying to act like you're being a hero?"

"No," he says. "I'm not being a hero. Though, whether you believe it or not, I actually like your father. And I don't have any desire to see the two of you out on the street. Even though you've been a pain in my ass ever since I moved up here."

"Then why are you doing this?" I ask.

"It's a good goddamned question, Avery. Maybe because you're my neighbors, and have been for five years and it's about the longest I've ever had neighbors." He looks at me, and my whole body feels warm. "Come over tomorrow morning. We'll have a talk."

"I don't want to talk to you."

"The fact that you're standing out here running your mouth seems to suggest otherwise."

"I don't—"

"Quiet," he says. "I'm done with it. I'm done with your attitude, I'm done with you. Go inside. Come up to my place tomorrow, and we'll talk."

Something in me goes quiet, and I want to resist it. All of it. I feel myself pushing back against the need rising up inside of me to obey him.

I have to keep this sexual psychosis contained.

There's a place for it, and it's not here, not with him.

"Go inside. Be a good girl."

It's like an arrow straight between my legs. Right where I feel myself starting to ache when I look at him. I tell myself that I'm only obeying him because that's the actual surprise. That I'd do what he said instead of arguing, and I'd rather surprise him.

Then I go upstairs without speaking to my father and slammed the door shut behind me.

I spend the whole rest of the night going over every problematic interaction I've ever had with him.

Caleb Flynn.

He's from here, originally. Though, I don't remember him from before. Probably because he's somewhere around fifteen years older than me, so I have no reason to. A foster kid, who went off and got rich doing something with luxury resort development. He's a billionaire. Came back and bought land looking over the town to make a point, I would think.

He moved into that big house on the hill. Then my dad sold him half our ranch. He put dad under a lot of pressure and my mom had just left for the third and final time so it was a rough run of luck for us.

I was livid. More than that I felt reckless – something I never was. Something I could never afford to be. But my life was falling apart, and he felt like a good target for my anger.

He caught me, grabbed hold of me and slammed me up against the side of that barn, hands tight around my wrists. It had felt like a fight.

And it had felt like sex, for all an eighteen-year-old virgin could know what sex felt like.

All that rage directed against me, the fierce control of his strength. The way his large hands had directed my movements. I felt powerless.

He could have done anything he wanted to me in that moment, and instead of fear I'd felt…

Turned on.

"You get the hell out of here," he'd said. "And give thanks that nobody got hurt, and that I'm not calling the police on you. You fucking brat."

His words stuck with me. And even now, they meld into my fantasies, twisting themselves up in my head and turning into something else.

"Fucking brat." He says that to me while he moves his hand from my wrist to my throat…

And I get off on it. Every time. Every time I see him I feel an explosion of heat that's not solely about hatred.

It fills me with shame. Then a deep sense of fear. It's what's been driving me the last few months. As pressure on the ranch has been building, it's been pushing me toward the thing I've been avoiding figuring out about myself.

Instead of sleeping I open up The Club app, which has

become the dirtiest of my dirty secrets. I've been going over and over my desires for a while now. Why every interaction I have with men leaves me so unsatisfied. I blame Caleb, actually. That interaction that we had when I was young. The way he held me, the way he used his strength against me. It's like it broke something in me. Like it turned me into a monster that I don't even recognize.

And it's finally driven me to this.

There aren't very many experienced Dominants in rural Oregon.

I've been considering actually experimenting with BDSM for a while. There's no one I can talk to about it. Not here. All of my friends would be utterly and completely scandalized, and then they'd be afraid.

For me, for my sanity. Afraid I'm like my mom because obviously she's a slut and therefore I must be drawn toward slut behavior because of her.

I'd be lying if I said that didn't get twisted up inside me sometimes. As far as I know, my mom's thing isn't kink (God, I never want to know what her thing is) it seemed like it had more to do with just wanting to get away from my dad.

But I can't deny that it puts me in a weird shame place. I tried. I tried to want a nice, normal guy who gave the potential of a nice, normal life and nice, normal sex and I blew that up three months ago.

After he proposed.

I panicked. Like a spooked horse trying to escape a barn.

I had felt like I loved Jon but then it just felt like more responsibility piled on top of everything I was already dealing with and I couldn't bear it. I wanted to feel like someone could take care of me, which is a simultaneously terrifying thought since I'd have to trust them in order to do that, and I don't trust anyone like that.

How can I?

Which is why this is a fantasy, though one I've been edging closer to making real. If I could pull the trigger.

My research has led me down a whole lot of rabbit holes and I've nearly leapt into a few really sketchy choices. I looked into physical sex clubs, but I don't like the idea of doing anything *in front* of anyone. Plus, I would have to travel to a bigger city, and that already feels scary given that I've so rarely been outside my home town.

I want a little secret trouble. I don't want big bad trouble where your body ends up floating in the Columbia because you went for an orgasm and got serial killed instead. No thanks.

I've always been good. Because I *have* to be. Because if I'm not good, then the ranch is going to fall apart. My parents were dissolute and irresponsible – though to give my dad his due, he's still here.

The one time I ever misbehaved was when I sneaked onto Caleb's land and nearly burned his barn to the ground. As misbehavior went, it was relatively spectacular.

But it wasn't BDSM club spectacular.

But that's how I ended up finding The Club app, during a desperate Google search that went something like How Do I Find a Dom Who Won't Kill Me If I Also Don't Want to Get Railed In Front of a Room Full of Strangers.

They really do have apps for everything.

It's dedicated to helping kinky people find a partner in their area who matches their personal needs.

Everyone is vetted, their identities verified, and there's a lot of built-in protection in that. People have STD tests on file, and their actual government names, even though you don't see them when you're chatting in the app.

The people running it know, and if something was going

to happen to you, they would know where you were, who you met with. There's just a whole lot of security built-in, and I like that.

I think.

Of course, I am also still terrified. I've only been with the one man and I assumed I'd marry him because part of me wanted to slip into an easy partnership that had some security.

The truth is, in action, I've always been the one in charge during sex too. I can't get out of my own head and I like directing things because it feels easier, safer.

The really weird thing about my BDSM fixation, my fantasies about being powerless, about being forced…is that it's nothing I've even come close to doing in real life. It's nothing I would say fits my personality at all.

BDSM is not a quick fuck. And I'm aware of that. There's something about it that terrifies me. The idea of giving my control away.

It's a particular kind of fear. One that attracts me more than it repulses me.

But the truth is, none of the sex that I've had has sparked the kind of need in me that that one angry encounter I had with Caleb has. The way he held me, his hands around my wrists like manacles. I'm intrigued by it.

I swallow hard, and open up the two dom profiles that I've been eyeing on the app.

There's one guy who lives local whose into pain. Pain and rough sex, which intrigues me, I'm not going to lie. But it's not *quite* what I'm after.

That very thought makes me laugh at myself. What am I after? Who can say. It's not like I know.

I swipe away from that profile and look at the next. He goes by The Duke and I'm not sure if that's a John Wayne reference – which I wouldn't know if my grandma hadn't been obsessed with him – or if he's trying to get the girls who are into Bridgerton, I can't work that one out. I'm not sure I need to.

He's into bondage. Elaborate knots and a total surrender of control. Dubious consent role-play.

Every time I read those words I start getting hot.

And I am intrigued in spite of myself. Mainly because nothing scares me more than the idea of losing control, and there's something that's so attractive to me about the idea that I could flirt with a loss of control while also having all these firm agreements in place.

It feels like something I could keep control over in a way. Something that I could maintain a grip on.

Just looking at the words in his profile starts to ramp up my libido. I've messaged him twice. He knows that I live in the area and that I'm an inexperienced submissive.

He told me that he likes to train subs who are trying to get into the lifestyle.

Just that word, *training*, that should make me mad. But it doesn't.

I think about messaging him, but instead I just read over our previous interactions.

I like to train submissives. Teach them to take everything I can give. Show them their limits.

I put my hand between my legs and start to touch myself. Everything is terrible, honestly. But this fantasy, this fantasy that I will probably never act on fuels me now. It makes me feel like everything isn't terrible.

I put my fist in my mouth as I bring myself to the peak with record speed.

God. Just thinking about him, this man that I've never seen…

It pushes me right over the edge. But I would be lying if I didn't say that I was imagining those cool blue eyes looking at me as I shudder out my orgasm.

I grit my teeth and throw my arm over my face. As long as I don't think about that tomorrow when I have to face him, I'll be fine.

Lucky, I'm practiced at that. Lucky that when I'm actually around him, the hatred usually takes over.

But for tonight, I'm just going to let myself relax into my sexual satisfaction.

I don't have anything else for me. Nothing else but this.

So I'm going to hold it close while I can.

Get it here:

Bound and Branded by Maisey Yates

ALSO BY JACKIE ASHDENDEN

Buy Links for all books: www.jackieashenden.com

STANDALONES

FALLING For Finn
    One Night With The Master (formerly Black Knight, White Queen) (Ebook only)

SERIES

THE LIES We Tell
    Taking Him
    Having Her

. . .

Hard Discipline

FORBIDDEN Desires
- Living In Shadow
- Living In Sin
- Living In Secret

TALKING DIRTY (EBOOK/AUDIO only)
- Talking Dirty With The CEO
- Talking Dirty With The Player
- Talking Dirty With The Boss

THE NINE CIRCLES
- Mine To Take
- Make You Mine
- You Are Mine
- Kidnapped By The Billionaire
- In Bed With The Billionaire

MOTOR CITY ROYALS
- Dirty For Me
- Wrong For Me
- Sin For Me

BAD BOY SHEIKHS (Ebook only)
- Never Seduce A Sheikh
- Never Refuse A Sheikh
- Never Resist A Sheikh

TEXAS BOUNTY

Cold Hearted Sniper (formerly Take Me Deeper)
Make It Hurt (ebook only)
Take Me Harder (ebook only)
The Hitman Next Door
Big Bad Marine
Black Sheep Bounty Hunter

TATE BROTHERS (BILLIONAIRE Navy SEALS)
The Dangerous Billionaire
The Wicked Billionaire
The Undercover Billionaire

11TH HOUR (ROMANTIC SUSPENSE)
Raw Power
Total Control
Hard Night

ALASKA HOMECOMING (sexy small town)
Come Home to Deep River
Deep River Promise
That Deep River Feeling

SMALL TOWN DREAMS (NZ set small town)
Find Your Way Home
All Roads Lead To You
Right Where We Belong

ARCADIA SERIES (erotic age-gap billionaire romance)

. . .

Tamed
    Bought
    Owned

Harlequin Dare (erotic romance)

Ruined
    Destroyed

King's Price
    King's Rule
    King's Ransom

The Debt

Dirty Devil
    Sexy Beast
    Bad Boss

In the Dark
    With The Lights On

Harlequin Presents
    Demanding His Hidden Heir

Claiming His One Night Child
Crowned At the Desert King's Command
The Spaniard's Wedding Revenge
Promoted to His Princess
The Most Powerful of Kings
The Italian's Final Redemption
The World's Most Notorious Greek
The Innocent Carrying His Legacy
The Wedding Night They Never Had
Pregnant by the Wrong Prince
The Innocent's One Night Proposal
A Diamond for My Forbidden Bride
Stolen for My Spanish Scandal
The Maid The Greek Married
Wed For Their Royal Heir
Her Vow To Be His Desert Queen

NOVELLAS

SERIES

BILLIONAIRE'S CLUB NYC (Ebook only)
  The Billion Dollar Bachelor
  The Billion Dollar Bad Boy
  The Billionaire Biker

BOXED SET OF ABOVE: 100 Shades Hotter edition

Billionaire Fairy Tales (Ebook only)

The Billionaire's Virgin
The Billionaire Beast
The Billionaire's Intern
The Big Bad Billionaire

MULTI-AUTHOR SERIES

HOLLYWOOD BLACKMAIL (SEACLIFF Medical series)

HOLD Me Down (Deacons of Bourbon Street biker series)

FRANKIE (SECRET CONFESSIONS: Down and Dusty)

A COWBOY For All Seasons
    A Good Old Fashioned Cowboy
    Sweet Home Cowboy
    The Comeback Cowboy